MILDRED AT ROSELANDS

The Original Mildred Classics

Mildred Keith

Mildred at Roselands

Mildred and Elsie

Mildred's Married Life

Mildred at Home

Mildred's Boys and Girls

Mildred's New Daughter

MILDRED AT ROSELANDS

Book Two of
The Original Mildred Classics

MARTHA FINLEY

CUMBERLAND HOUSE
NASHVILLE, TENNESSEE

MILDRED AT ROSELANDS
by Martha Finley

Any unique characteristics of this edition:
Copyright © 2001 by Cumberland House Publishing, Inc.

Published by Cumberland House Publishing, Inc.,
431 Harding Industrial Drive, Nashville, Tennessee 37211.

Cover design by Bruce Gore, Gore Studios, Inc.
Photography by Dean Dixon Photography
Hair and Makeup by Calene Rader
Text design by Julie Pitkin

ISBN: 1-58182-228-6

Printed in the United States of America
1 2 3 4 5 6 7 8 — 05 04 03 02 01

Mildred at Roselands

PREFACE

A sweet attractive kinde of grace,
A full assurance given by lookes,
Continuall comfort in a face
The lineaments of Gospell bookes.

—MATTHEW ROYDON

MY STORY MAY seem to end somewhat abruptly, but it is to be continued in a future volume. The date of this tale is about four years earlier than that of *Elsie Dinsmore*—the first of the *Elsie* series—and anyone who cares to know more of the little heiress of Viamede will find the narrative of her life carried on in those books.

—M.F.

CHAPTER FIRST

Prayer ardent opens heaven.

—YOUNG

IT WAS NEAR NOON of a bright, warm day early in October. Mrs. Keith was alone in her pretty sitting room, busily plying her needle at the open window looking out upon the river.

Occasionally she lifted her head and sent a quick, admiring glance at its bright, swiftly flowing waters and the woods beyond—beautiful and gorgeous in their rich autumnal robes.

There was a drowsy hum of insects in the air, and mingling with it the cackle of a rejoicing hen, the crowing of a cock, and other rural sounds. The prattle of childish voices, too, came pleasantly to her ear from the garden behind the house where the little ones were at play. It brought once again a tender, motherly smile to her lips.

Yet a slight cloud of care rested on her usually calm and placid features, and thought seemed very busy in her brain.

It was of Mildred she was thinking. Father and mother both had noticed, with a good deal of anxiety that the young girl did not recover fully from the severe strain of the long weeks of nursing that had been her lot during the past summer.

She was much paler and thinner than her wont, had frequent headaches, and seemed weak and languid, a very little exertion causing excessive fatigue.

Only last night they had lain awake an hour or more talking about it and consulting together as to what could be done for the "dear child."

They feared the severity of the coming winter would increase her malady and wished very much that they could send her away for some months, or a year, to a milder climate. But the difficulty— apparently an insuperable one—was to find the means.

It took no small amount of the same to feed, clothe, and educate such a family as theirs, and sickness had made this year one of unusual expense.

As the loving mother sat there alone, she had turned over in her mind plan after plan for accomplishing this, which for her child's good she so ardently desired to do. But each idea in turn was rejected as utterly impracticable.

Aunt Wealthy, she knew, would gladly take Mildred into her pleasant home for as long a time as her parents might be willing to spare her, but still there was the money to be provided for the journey. Besides, an even milder climate than that of Lansdale was desirable.

But the slight cloud lifted from Mrs. Keith's brow, and a sweet expression of perfect peace and contentment took its place as she thought of her best Friend and His infinite love and power. He could clear away all these difficulties and would do so in answer to prayer, if in His unerring wisdom He saw that it would be for their real good—their truest happiness.

Her heart went up to Him in a silent petition, and a sweet, glad song of praise burst half unconsciously from her lips.

As she ceased, a rap at the door into the hall—which, as well as the outer one, stood wide open—caught her ear.

She turned her head to see a tall gentleman, a fine-looking, middle-aged man, standing there and regarding her with a pleased smile.

"Uncle Dinsmore! Is it possible? Oh, how glad I am to see you!" she cried, dropping her work and springing toward him with both hands extended.

He took them and drew her to him, kissing her quite affectionately, first on one cheek, then on the other. He said, merrily, "I flattered myself you would be, else I should not have traveled some hundreds of miles for the express purpose of paying you a visit. Fair and sweet as ever, Marcia! Time deals more gently with you than is his wont with most of the world."

"Ah, I remember you as always given to pretty compliments," she returned with a pleased but half-incredulous smile as she drew forward the most comfortable chair in the room and made him seat himself therein, while she relieved him of his hat and cane.

"So I have taken you by great surprise?" he said inquiringly and with a satisfied look.

"I did not even know you were in the North. When did you leave Roselands? Were they all well? Are any of them with you?"

"One question at a time, Marcia," he said with a good-humored laugh. "I left home in June, bringing all the family with me as far as Philadelphia. They are visiting now in eastern Pennsylvania. I went on to New York a month ago to see Horace off to Europe, then decided to come on to Ohio and Indiana to have a look at this great western country, your Aunt Wealthy, and yourself. I purpose to spend a week or two with you, if quite convenient and agreeable, then to return by way of Lansdale and paying a short visit there."

"Convenient and agreeable!" she cried with a joyous laugh, glad tears shining in her eyes. "Sunlight was never more welcome, and the longer you stay, the better. You came by stage? Where is your luggage?"

"Yes, by the stage. My valise is—Ah!" he said, half rising from his chair, with had extended, as a handsome, intelligent-looking lad of fifteen or sixteen came in from the hall, carrying a valise.

"I found this on the porch," he began, but he broke off abruptly at sight of the stranger.

"Rupert, our eldest son," said Mrs. Keith with a glance full of motherly pride directed toward the lad. Rupert, this is Uncle Dinsmore, Cousin Horace's father."

The two shook hands warmly, Rupert saying, "I

am very glad to see you, sir. I have heard mother speak of you so often."

The gentleman answered, "Thank you, my boy. Yes, your mother and I are very old friends, though I am older than she by a score of years or more."

"That must be your uncle's, Rupert, take it to the spare room," said Mrs. Keith, glancing at the valise.

"A fine looking fellow, but he's all Keith, isn't he, Marcia?" remarked her uncle as the lad left the room. Then, as Cyril bounded in at another door, he said, "Ah! This one's a Stanhope! Come and shake hands with your uncle, my man."

Don and the two girls were close behind, and Mr. Keith came in shortly after that from his office, bringing with him Mildred, Zillah, and Ada, whom he had met on the way.

Mr. Dinsmore was a stranger to them all, but everyone seemed glad that he had come to visit them. He was quite charmed with the cordiality of his reception, the bright, intelligent faces, and the refined manners of both parents and children.

They made him very welcome, very comfortable, and spared no exertion for his entertainment.

Being an observant man, he soon discovered that Mildred, toward whom he felt especially drawn from the first, was ailing, and he immediately proposed to take her home with him to spend the winter in the sunny South.

This was on the afternoon of the day succeeding that of his arrival, as he and Mr. and Mrs. Keith sat conversing together in the parlor, the young people having scattered to their work or play.

The father and mother exchanged glances, each reading in the other's face a longing desire to accept the invitation for their child but mingled with the sad conviction that it was impossible to do so.

This Mr. Keith presently put into words accompanied with warm thanks for the intended kindness to Mildred.

"Tut, tut," said Mr. Dinsmore, "don't talk of kindness. The obligation will be on my part and as to the impossibility, it is all in your imagination. I, of course, shall bear all the expense of the journey, and—No, Marcia, don't interrupt me. I owe it to you, for I can never repay the kindness you showed your aunt in her last sickness and to poor Horace and myself after she was gone. And you owe it to your child not to refuse for her what is really necessary to her restoration to health."

"Dear uncle, you are most kind. You must let me say it," said Mrs. Keith with tears in her eyes. "I will not deny that the expense is the greatest obstacle, for the family purse is low at present, and I will not let my pride stand in the way of the acceptance of your generous offer. But there are other difficulties. I do not see how I could get her ready in the few days to which you have limited your visit here."

"I'll stretch it to a fortnight, then, if that'll answer," he returned in a short, quick, determined way that indicated he was little used to opposition to his will. "Besides," he went on, "what need is there for so much preparation? Purchases can be made to much better advantage in Philadelphia, and the sewing can be done at Roselands, where we have two accom-

plished seamstresses among the servants. I've heard
Mrs. Dinsmore boast that one of them can cut and
fit, make and trim a dress as well as any dressmaker
she ever saw."

Mrs. Keith expressed a lively sense of his kindness
but suggested that in all probability Mrs. Dinsmore
found plenty of employment for the two women in
sewing for herself and the family.

Her uncle scouted the idea, asserting that they had
not enough to do to keep them out of mischief.

Mrs. Keith was driven from her last refuge of
excuse, and truth to tell, was not sorry to leave it so.
Mr. Keith gave consent. Mildred was summoned,
and the plan laud before her to her great astonishment and delight.

"Oh, Uncle Dinsmore, how kind!" she exclaimed,
her cheeks flushing and her eyes sparkling. "It seems
too good to be true that I shall see Roselands—that
beautiful place mother has so often described to us!
But no, no, it will never do for me to go and leave
mother to bear the cares and burdens of housekeep-
ing and the children all alone!" she cried with a sudden change of tone.

"How could I be so selfish as to think of it for a single moment? Mother, dear, I don't want to go.
Indeed, I do not."

"But my dear child, I want you to go," Mrs. Keith
said, smiling through unshed tears. "You need rest
and a change of scene. Though I shall miss you sadly,
I shall enjoy the thought that you are gaining in
many ways, and in the prospect of soon having you
at home again."

"Yes," said Mr. Dinsmore, "travel is improving, and you can go on with your studies at Roselands if you fancy doing so. We have an excellent, thoroughly educated lady as governess, and masters come from the city twice a week to give instruction in music and drawing. You shall share their attentions if you will.

"Come, it is not worthwhile to raise objections, for I can overrule them all and am quite determined to carry my point.

"Mr. Keith," he added, rising and looking about for his hat, "suppose we take a walk around the town, leaving these ladies to talk over the necessary arrangements."

The gentlemen went out together, but the next moment, Mr. Dinsmore stepped back again to hand Mrs. Keith a letter, saying as he did so, "I owe you an apology, Marcia, for my forgetfulness. Horace entrusted this to my care, and it should have been given to you immediately on my arrival. *Au revoir*, ladies!" he said, and with a courtly bow, he was gone.

Mrs. Keith broke the seal and unfolded the sheet. There was an enclosure, but she did not look at it until she had read the note, which she did almost at a glance, for it was plainly written and very brief.

Dear Marcia,
Excuse a hasty line, as I am going aboard the steamer which is to carry me to Europe.
I know my father wants to take Mildred with him on his return to Roselands. I hope you will

16

let her go, and that you will do me the great kindness of accepting the enclosed trifle to be used in providing her with an outfit such as you deem suitable. It is a very small part of the debt I have owed you ever since the death of my loved mother.

> Your affectionate cousin,
> Horace Dinsmore

"The dear, generous fellow!" she exclaimed, tears starting to her eyes. Then, as she unfolded the bank note, she said, "A trifle, indeed! Mildred, child, it is a hundred dollars!" The tears rolled down her cheeks.

"But you will not take it, mother, surely!" said Mildred, her cheeks flushing hotly and her pride up in arms at once at the thought of coming under such an obligation, even to a relative.

"My child," said Mrs. Keith, "I could not bear to hurt him, and I well know he would be hurt by a rejection of his kindness. We will accept it—if not as a gift, as a loan to be repaid someday when we are able. Another reason why I feel that we ought not to let pride lead us to refuse this is that it seems to have come—it and your uncle's invitation also—so directly in answer to prayer."

She went on to tell Mildred of their anxiety in regard to her, and in particular of the petitions she had been putting up on her behalf, just before Mr. Dinsmore's arrival.

"Ah!" she said in conclusion, "how good is our God! He has fulfilled to me His gracious promise, 'And it shall come to pass that before they call, I will answer, and while they are yet speaking, I will hear.'"

A moment's silence followed, then Mildred said in half-tremulous tones, "Oh, it is a blessed thing to trust God! I hope my faith will grow to be as strong as yours, mother, and I hope I am thankful for this money. But—mother, am I very wicked to feel it something of a trial to have to take it?"

"I hope not," Mrs. Keith answered with a smile and a sigh. "I do not want to see my children too ready to take help from others. I trust they will always prefer any honest work by which they may earn their bread to a life of luxury and ease and dependence. I hope that they will always remember the command, 'Every man shall bear his own burden.'

"But since we are also told to bear one another's burdens and that it is more blessed to give than to receive, I must believe there are cases where it is right—yes, even a duty—to accept some assistance from those who give freely and gladly and from their abundance, as I know Cousin Horace does."

"Well, I must try not to be so selfish as to begrudge him his blessedness," remarked Mildred playfully, though tears still shone in her eyes. "But, mother, how are you to do without me?"

"Oh, very nicely! Zillah and Ada are growing very helpful. Annis is no longer a mere baby, and—why, there is Celestia Ann!" she exclaimed joyously, suddenly breaking off her sentence, as a casual glance through a window showed her the tall, muscular figure of their former and most efficient maid-of-all-work coming in at the gate.

"Oh! If she has only come to stay, I shall feel as if I can be spared!" cried Mildred. "Mother, how strange it is that difficulties are being taken out of the way."

CHAPTER SECOND

'Tis you alone can save, or give my doom.

—OVID

CELESTIA ANN HAD come to stay if wanted, of which in her secret soul she had no doubt, want of self-appreciation not being one of her failings. She knew her own value quite as well as did anyone else.

"If you've got a girl and don't want me," she remarked, upon announcing her errand, "it don't make no difference. I'm not perticler about workin' out this fall. If I was, there's places enough. Though I am free to admit I feel a leetle more at home here than anywheres else and set great store by you all."

"We have a girl," said Mrs. Keith, "but she leaves us in another week, and in the meanwhile, I shall be glad to have two, as Mildred and I will be very busy with the preparations for her journey."

"Journey! Is she goin' off? 'Tain't on her weddin' trip, is it? I heerd there was talk of her gettin' married, and I said then I was bound to have a finger in that pie—makin' the weddin' cake."

"Oh, no, she's quite too young for that yet," Mrs. Keith said with a slight smile. "She's only going South on a visit to some relations."

21

"I want you to promise to stay and take care of mother and the rest till I come back, Celestia Ann," added Mildred.

"Well, you've got to promise first that you'll not stay forever," prudently stipulated Miss Hunsinger. "When do you plan to come back?"

"Next spring."

"Hmm—well, I won't mind engagin' for that length of time provided my folks at home keeps well, so's I'm not needed there."

"Then it's a bargain?" queried Mildred joyously.

"Yes, I reckon."

And Celestia Ann hung up her sunbonnet behind the kitchen door and set to work at once with her wonted energy, while Mrs. Keith and Mildred withdrew to the bedroom of the latter to examine the condition of her wardrobe and consult as to needed repairs and additions.

They quickly decided that no new dresses should be purchased and very little shopping of any kind done until her arrival in Philadelphia, as she could buy to much better advantage there and learn what were the prevailing fashions before having the goods made up.

Mrs. Keith had never made dress a matter of primary importance with herself or with her children, but she thought it well enough to conform to the fashions sufficiently to avoid being conspicuous for singularity of attire.

"We must give thought enough to the matter to decide how our clothes are to be made," she said. "And it is easier to follow the prevailing style than to contrive something different for ourselves, provided it be pretty and becoming, for I think it a duty we owe our friends to look as well as we can."

And on this principle, she was desirous that Mildred's dress should be entirely suitable to her age and station, and handsome and fashionable enough to ensure she would be neither eyesore nor annoyance to Mrs. Dinsmore, whose guest she was to be.

"The fashions are so slow in reaching these western towns that I know we must be at least a year or two behind," she remarked in a lively tone, as she turned over and examined Mildred's best dress—a pretty blue-black silk, almost as good as new. "That doesn't trouble me so long as we are at home, but I don't want you to look outré to our relations and their friends, because that would be a mortification to them as well as to yourself. So, though this is perfectly good, I think it will be best to try to match it and have it remodeled."

"Mother," said Mildred, "when it comes to buying dresses for myself, how I shall miss you! I'm afraid I shall make some sad mistakes."

The young girl looked really troubled and anxious as she spoke, and her mother answered in a kindly reassuring tone, "I am not at all afraid to trust to your taste or judgment, so you need not be."

"But I shall not know where to go to find what I want or whether the price asked is a fair one."

"Well, my dear child, even these trifling cares and anxieties we may carry to our kind heavenly Father, feeling sure that a way will be provided out of the difficulty. Probably your aunt or uncle, or some other friend, will go with you."

The mother's tone was so cheerful and confident that Mildred caught her spirit and grew merry and light-hearted over her preparations.

Although the dressmaking was deferred, there was still enough to be done in the few days of the allotted time to keep both mother and daughter very busy, which was just as well, as it left them no leisure to grieve over the approaching separation.

The news that she was going so far away and to be absent so long created some consternation in the little coterie to which Mildred belonged.

Claudina Chetwood and Lu Grange declared themselves almost inconsolable, while Wallace Ormsby was privately of the opinion that their loss was as nothing compared to his.

Months ago, he had decided that life would be a desert without Mildred to share it with him. But he had never found courage to tell her so, for he feared the feeling was not reciprocated and that she had only a friendly liking for him.

He had hoped to win her heart in time, but now the opportunity was to be taken from him and given to others. It was not a cheerful prospect, and Mildred was so busy there seemed no chance of getting a word alone with her.

"My mother tells me you are going away, Mildred, on a long journey and for a lengthened stay?" Mr. Lord remarked inquiringly and with a regretful tone in his voice as he shook hands with her after the weekly evening service.

He had been absent from town for a week or two.

"Yes," she returned merrily, putting aside with determination the thought of the partings that must wrench her heart at the last. "I am all ready, trunk packed and everything, and I expect to start tomorrow morning."

"Ah, it's quite unfortunate. We shall miss you sadly. May I—"

But someone called to him from the other side of the room. He was obliged to turn away without finishing his sentence, and Wallace Ormsby seized the opportunity to step up and offer his arm to Mildred.

She accepted it, and they walked on in silence till they were quite out of earshot of the rest of the small congregation.

Then Wallace opened his lips to speak, but the words he wanted would not come. He could only stammer out a trite remark about the weather.

"Yes, it's beautiful," said Mildred. "I do hope it will last so, at least till we reach the Wabash. However, we will go in a covered vehicle, and I suppose we will not get wet even if it should rain."

"I wish you weren't going!" cried Wallace impetuously. "No, not that either, for I think, I hope, the journey will do you good. But—oh, Mildred, I cannot bear the thought that you may—that somebody else will win you away from me. I—I don't presume to say that I have any right, but I love you dearly and always shall, and I do think I could make you happy if you only could return it." He went on speaking fast, now that he had found his tongue. "Oh, Mildred, do you think you could?"

"I don't know, Wallace," she said, her voice trembling a little. "I have a very great respect and esteem for you—affection, too," she added with some hesitation, feeling the hot blood surge over her face at the words. "But I don't think it's quite the sort you want."

"You love somebody else?" he whispered hoarsely.

"No, no. There is no one I like better than I do you. But we are both very young and—"

"Perhaps you might learn to like me in time?" he queried eagerly, tremulously, as one hoping even against hope.

"Yes, though I do *like* you now. But it ought to be something stronger, you know, and I couldn't make any promises now, and neither must you."

"I should be glad to," he said, "for I am perfectly certain I should never repent."

He bade her goodnight at the gate, saying he would not make it good-bye if he might come to see her off in the morning.

"Certainly, Wallace," she said. "You are like one of the family. You have seemed that to all of us ever since your great kindness to us last summer."

"Don't speak of it," he answered hastily. "You conferred a great obligation in allowing me, for it was one of my greatest pleasure in life to be permitted to share your burdens."

26

CHAPTER THIRD

How poor a thing is pride!

—DANIEL

THE PARTING WAS no slight trial to her who went or to those who stayed behind, particularly the loving, tender mother. But both she and Mildred bore it bravely, though the heart of the latter almost failed her as she felt the clinging arms of the little ones about her neck, heard their sobs, and saw their tears and again, as she found herself clasped to her father's and then to her mother's breast with many a fond caress and low-breathed words of farewell and affection.

Wallace wrung her hand with a whispered a passionate entreaty: "Oh, Mildred, darling, don't forget me! I'll remember you to the day of my death."

The weather was fine, the air crisp, cool, and bracing, and when the town and a few miles of prairies had been left behind, their way led through woods beautiful with all the rich tints of October's most lavish mood.

Mr. Dinsmore exerted himself to be entertaining, and ere long he and Mildred were chatting and laughing right merrily.

They took their dinner at a farmhouse newly built on a little clearing in the forest, finding themselves not daintily served but supplied with an abundance of good, substantial, well-cooked food—bread, butter, coffee, ham and eggs, and two or three kinds of vegetables, with stewed dried-apple pie for dessert.

After an hour's rest for themselves and horses, they traveled on again, reaching a little town in time to get their supper and a night's lodging at its tavern, where the fare and accommodations were on a par with those of the farmhouse.

They had found the roads rough. Those they passed over the next day were worse still, mostly corduroy, over the rounded logs of which the wheels passed with constant jolting. Where a log had been displaced or rotted away, as was occasionally the case, there would be a sudden descent of first the fore, then the hind wheels, with a violent jerk that nearly threw them from their seats.

They reached Delphi on the Wabash, where they were to take a steamboat, sore, weary, and very glad to make the change.

A night was spent at the Delphi hotel, and the next morning, they went aboard the boat, which carried them down the Wabash and up the Ohio to Madison, where they landed again and passed part of a day and night. Embarking once more in a larger craft, they continued on their way up the Ohio as far as Portsmouth, whence a stage carried them across the country to Lansdale.

Miss Stanhope had not received the letter that should have informed her of their coming. She was sitting alone by the fire, quietly knitting and thinking of the dear ones far away in Pleasant Plains, when the long and prolonged "Toot! Toot!" of a horn, followed by the roll and rumble of wheels, aroused her from her reverie.

"The evening stage," she said half aloud. Then she rose hastily, dropping her knitting, and hurried to the door, for surely it had stopped at her gate.

Yes, there it was. A gentleman had alighted and was handing out a lady, while the guard was at the boot getting out their trunks. She could see it all plainly in the moonlight, as she threw the door to the house wide open.

"Who can they be?" she asked herself, as she stepped quickly across the porch and down the garden path to meet and welcome her unexpected guests.

The next moment, Mildred's arms were about her neck, and both were weeping for joy.

"Dear child, this is a glad surprise!" cried Miss Stanhope, straining the young girl to her breast. "But where are the rest?"

"Here. I'm the only other one, Sister Wealthy," said Mr. Dinsmore, lifting his hat with one hand, while the other one was held out to her. "Haven't you a word of welcome for me?"

"Arthur Dinsmore, my brother-in-law!" she cried, taking the hand and offering him her lips. "I was never more surprised or delighted!

"Come in, come in, both of you. You must be cold, tired, and hungry. I hope you've come to make a long stay. Simon will carry in the trunks," she went on rapidly as she seized Mildred's hand and led the way to the house, simply beside herself with the sudden delight of seeing them.

She had many questions to ask, but the comfort of the weary travelers was the first thing to be attended to. She removed Mildred's wraps with her own hands, rejoicing over her all the while as a mother might do over a lost child restored. She would have done the same by Mr. Dinsmore if he had waited for her.

She soon had each cozily seated in a comfortable armchair beside the blazing fire, with Simon kindling fires in the spare rooms and Phillis busy in the kitchen, preparing a tempting meal.

"You couldn't be more welcome than you are, brother, or you, Mildred, my dear child," she said, coming back from overseeing all these matters. "But you might have fared better, perhaps, if you had sent word that you were coming."

"I wrote from Pleasant Plains," he answered. "The letter has been either lost or delayed in the mails."

"Ah, well, we won't fret about it," she responded cheerily. "I, at least am far too happy to fret about anything," she added, feasting her eyes upon Mildred's face.

"Dear child, you are quite worn and thin!" she exclaimed presently, her eyes filling. "That nursing was far too hard for you. How I wish I could have saved you from some of it, but you have come to stay all winter with me and have a good rest. Haven't you?"

"No, no, she belongs to me for the winter," interposed Mr. Dinsmore before Mildred could open her lips to reply. "If you want her company, Sister

Wealthy, you must make up your mind to be our guest also. What is to hinder you from shutting up your house and going with us to Roselands? I am sure I need not say that we would be delighted to have you do so."

"You are very kind, brother," she said, giving him an affectionate look, "but there are reasons why it would not do for me to leave home for so long a visit. Where is Horace, my dear sister Eva's son? I wish he had come with you. Poor boy!" she added, sighing deeply.

A slight frown gathered on Mr. Dinsmore's brow at that. "He is hardly a subject for pity," he remarked. "He has just sailed for Europe with pleasant prospects before him and in apparently excellent spirits."

He looked fixedly at her, then glanced at Mildred, and taking the hint, she dropped the subject for that time.

She was at no loss for topics of conversation, so eager was she to learn all that could be told her in regard to the dear ones Mildred had left behind. Also, she felt a lively interest in the family at Roselands, though they were not actually related to her, being the children of the present Mrs. Dinsmore, who was the second wife and successor to Horace's mother.

Finding herself alone with Mr. Dinsmore the next day, Miss Stanhope said, "You tell me Horace has gone to Europe? Will he be long absent?"

"It is quite uncertain," he answered carelessly. "He may prolong his stay to a year or more."

"He has his child with him, I hope."

"His child!"

Mr. Dinsmore seemed much annoyed.

"Certainly not," he said after a moment's disturbed pause. "What could he do with her? But I really hoped you knew nothing about that ridiculous affair. Pray how did you learn of it?"

"Horace told Marcia and requested her to write the particulars to me," Aunt Wealthy answered meekly. "And is she still with her guardian, the poor dear?"

"Yes, and she will be, I trust, for years to come. That mad escapade of Horace's—for I can call his hasty, ill-timed, imprudent marriage by no other name—has been to me the continual source of untold mortification and annoyance."

"It was not a bad match except on account of their extreme youth?" Miss Stanhope said in a tone between assertion and inquiry.

"I consider it so most decidedly," he returned, his eyes kindling with anger. "Elsie Grayson, the daughter of a man who, though wealthy, had made all his money by trade, was no fit match for my son. I consider it a fortunate thing that she did not live. It would have been, in my estimation, still more fortunate if her child had died with her."

Miss Stanhope was shocked.

"Oh, Arthur, how can you?" she exclaimed, tears starting to her eyes. "How can you feel so toward your own little granddaughter—a poor motherless baby, too! Truly, pride must be a great hardener of the heart."

"Old Grayson's grandchild," he muttered, rising to pace the floor in a hasty, excited manner. "Please oblige me by not mentioning this subject again," he said. "It is exceedingly unpleasant to me."

Miss Stanhope sighed inwardly.

"Arthur," she said, "pride goeth before destruction, and a haughty spirit before a fall."

She did not broach the subject again during the remainder of his brief stay with her.

"I am going out for a look at your town," he said, taking up his hat. "I hope," he added, turning back at the door with his hand on the knob, "that Mildred has heard nothing of this affair?"

"She knows all that I do, I believe," Miss Stanhope answered quietly. "It seemed to be Horace's wish that she should be told."

Mr. Dinsmore went out with a groan, and Mildred, coming in at that instant by another door, heard it and inquired somewhat anxiously of her aunt what was the matter.

Miss Stanhope thought it best to tell her and advise avoidance of any allusion to Horace's wife or child when in her uncle's presence, unless he should himself take the initiative.

Mildred promised to be careful. "Though why he should feel so, I cannot understand," she added. "I, for my part, feel the greatest interest in that little child and regret exceedingly that I shall not see her. But Cousin Horace's feelings toward her are more inexplicable still. How can he help loving his own little baby girl, who seems to have no one else to love and cherish her except the servants!"

It was now an hour since they had left the breakfast table. Miss Stanhope's morning duties, connected with the care of the household, had been attended to; Phillis and Simon had received their orders for the day; and the good lady might conscientiously indulge herself and Mildred in the lengthened chat both had been longing for ever since the arrival of the latter the previous night.

Of course, the first and most absorbingly interesting topic was the home circle at Pleasant Plains. That thoroughly discussed, they passed on to friends and neighbors both there and here, each finding numerous questions to ask the other and many bits of news to give.

"What has become of poor Mrs. Osborne and Frank?" Mildred inquired.

"Ah, she has gone home at last and is forever done with pain and sickness," Miss Stanhope answered. "It was hard for Frank but a blessed release to her — poor dear woman! It was three weeks ago she went, and a week later, Frank came to bid me good-bye. He's going to work his way through college, he told me, and make his mark in the world. And, Milly, my dear," she added with a slightly mischievous smile, "he hinted pretty broadly that when his laurels were won, they would be laid at the feet of a certain young girl of my acquaintance, if I thought there might be some faint hope that she would not deem it a presumption to do so."

"And what did you answer to that, Aunt Wealthy;" queried Mildred, with heightened color and a look of mingled vexation and amusement. "He is such a mere boy!" she added. "I never thought of him as anything else."

"Of course not, nor did I. But he is a good, true, noble fellow, bright and intelligent above the ordinary, and very modest and unassuming with it all. He will make a fine man."

"Yes. I think so, too, and if he happens to fancy one of my younger sisters, I'll consent with all my heart and do what I can to further his suit."

Aunt Wealthy shook her head and smiled. "That's not what he wants now, but who knows? Time does work wonderful changes now and then."

Mildred's thoughts seemed to have wandered away from the subject. She was silent for a moment, then suddenly asked, "Aunt Wealthy, do you know what sort of person— Dear me, what am I to call her? Mrs. Dinsmore? What would you do about it?"

"I should ask her what title she preferred and act accordingly. No, I have never met her and know very little about her, except that she is not at all considered a pious woman."

"And uncle?"

"Is not a Christian, either," Miss Stanhope said sorrowfully as Mildred paused, leaving her sentence unfinished. "He believes there is nothing more necessary to secure salvation than an honest, upright, and moral life. My dear child, you are going into an atmosphere of worldliness, and you will need to watch and pray, keeping close to the Master. Ah! What a joy it is that we need never be any farther away from Him in one place than in another!"

"Yes, that was what mother said," murmured Mildred, tears filling her eyes at the thought of the many miles now lying between her and that loved parent and friend. "She promised to pray daily for me that I might be kept from evil, and you will do so, too, Aunt Wealthy, will you not?"

"Indeed I will, dear child," was the earnest response.

Chapter Fourth

Wear this for me.

— Shakespeare

"Your traveling suit is very neat and quite becoming—very ladylike," Miss Stanhope remarked with an approving glance at Mildred's trim figure. "I don't think your Uncle Dinsmore can have felt that he had any reason to be ashamed of you."

"I hope not," was the smiling rejoinder, "and I did not see any indication of it."

"But how about the rest of your wardrobe, child? I fear you had a small choice of materials in Pleasant Plains and very little time for making up your purchases. We might do rather better here, if we could persuade your uncle to lengthen his intended stay."

"Thank you, auntie dear, you are always so kind and thoughtful," Mildred said. "But I don't think he could be persuaded, and indeed, I should not like to have him delay for my sake, because I know he and his wife are anxious to get home before the cold weather sets in."

She went on to explain her plans and to tell of her Cousin Horace's generous gift.

"That was just like him. He's an open-handed, noble fellow," was Aunt Wealthy's comment. "You need never hesitate to take a kindness from him, because he enjoys it and is abundantly able. But I must not be outdone by him," she continued with a smile, rising and going to her bureau, for they were in her bedroom now. "I wish to do my share in proportion to my ability."

Mildred protested that her wants were already well supplied, but playfully bidding her to be quiet and let older and wiser heads judge that, Miss Stanhope proceeded to take a key from her pocket, unlock the drawer of her bureau, and bring forth her treasures—a quantity of rich, old lace that the finest lady in the land might have been proud to wear, several handsome rings, a diamond pin, and a beautiful gold chain for the neck.

"They are old-fashioned, dearie," she said, "but no one will mistake them for pinchbeck and colored glass," she added with her low, musical laugh as she threw the chain about Mildred's neck and slipped the rings upon her fingers.

The girl's cheeks flushed, and her eyes sparkled.

"Oh, Aunt Wealthy," she cried, "how can you trust such treasures to my keeping? Old-fashioned, indeed! They are all the more delightful for that, showing that one does not belong to the mushroom gentry but to a good, substantial, old family. But you must not let me use them, lest they should be lost or stolen. I should be frightened out of my wits in either case."

"Nonsense, child! You would have no need, for the

loss would be more yours than mine. I shall never wear them again, and they will all belong, someday, to you or your sisters," Miss Stanhope said, turning to her bureau once more.

Lifting out something carefully wrapped in a towel, she laid it in Mildred's lap, saying, "This, too, you must take with you. You will want a handsome wrap in Philadelphia, before you can go out to buy, and this will serve the purpose even better than anything you would feel able to purchase. Won't it?" she queried with another of her sweet and silvery laughs.

Mildred fairly caught her breath in her delighted surprise.

"Oh, Aunt Wealthy, your beautiful India shawl! You can't mean to lend *that* to me!"

"That is just what I mean, Milly. Stand up a minute, dear" she answered merrily, taking it from its wrappings and draping it about the slender girlish figure. "There! Nothing could be more becoming. I can only lend, not give it, because it is already willed to your mother. But it is to descend always to the eldest daughter."

"Aunt Wealthy, I'm afraid to borrow it, afraid something might happen to it. So please, put it away again."

"Tut, child! Something might happen to it at home. Suppose the house should burn down with everything in it. Wouldn't I be glad the shawl was saved by being far away in your keeping?"

It was very rich and costly, and it was highly prized by Miss Stanhope as the gift of a favorite brother, long since dead. He had been a wanderer and had lived many years in China and India, from whence he had sent her, from time to time, rare and beautiful things, orf which this was one. At length, he came home to die in her arms, leaving her the bulk of his fortune—enough to make her very comfortable.

Her means were ample for her own needs but not for her abundant charities. She spent little on herself but gave with a liberal hand.

"Yes, I know you would, auntie," Mildred said, passing her hand caressingly over the soft, rich folds. "But in my wildest dreams, I never supposed you would lend this to me, and if I were in your place, I don't think I'd do it," she concluded with an arch look and smile.

"You are a careful little body, and I'm not afraid to trust you. You must carry it with you, my child, and wear it, too, as a favor to me. You can't suppose I feel willing to have Mrs. Dinsmore's aristocratic nose turn up at a niece of mine for lack of a little finery that lies idle in my bureau drawer?"

"Ah, if you put it on that score, I can't refuse," laughed Mildred, her face sparkling with pleasure. "Oh, but you're too good to let me have it! It is so handsome, auntie! It seems like a whole outfit in itself," she went on, dancing about the room in almost wild delight.

Then sobering down a little and standing before the glass to note the effect, she said, "I don't think that I have seen it a half a dozen times before—when worn on some grand occasion by you or mother— and it has always inspired me with a kind of awe as something to be looked at from a respectful distance and by no means handled. So it seems almost beyond belief that I am actually to wear it."

The few days Mr. Dinsmore had apportioned to their visit to Lansdale flew rapidly by—all too rapidly for Miss Stanhope, who was loath to part with them, Mildred especially But the young girl, full of youthful eagerness to see the world, was hardly sorry to go, in spite of her sincere affection for her aunt.

They returned to the Ohio River as they had come, striking it at the nearest point, where they once more embarked in a steamboat, taking passage for Pittsburgh.

They were again favored with pleasant weather, for the most of the time, and Mildred enjoyed the trip. Mr. Dinsmore was very kind and attentive to her comfort, and she made some rather agreeable acquaintances among her fellow passengers.

They dined and spent some hours at a hotel in Pittsburgh, then took the cars for Philadelphia.

This was a new mode of travel to Mildred and not what she would have chosen. She had read newspaper accounts of railroad accidents and felt, in going upon the train, that she was risking life and limb.

But she kept her fears to herself, determined not to be an annoyance to her uncle, and he never suspected how her heart was quaking as she took quiet possession of the seat he selected for her.

"We are early," he remarked with a glance about the almost empty car as he sat down beside her. Then, looking at his watch, he aded, "Yes, fully fifteen minutes to wait before the train starts. Well, that's a good deal better than being too late.

"Mildred, there's something I want to say to you before we join your aunt, and perhaps this is as good a time for it as any. There! Don't be alarmed,"he said as she gave him a startled look. "It's nothing unpleasant— only that I would rather you would not say anything to Mrs. Dinsmore about your father's circumstances. My dear, I am not meaning to wound your feelings," he added hastily, for she was blushing painfully and her eyes had filled.

"I think quite as much of him and of you all as if you were rolling in wealth. But my wife is—well, does not always see things so precisely as I do. It will make us more comfortable all around if she is left to suppose that your mother is still in possession of the fortune she once had."

He paused, and Mildred, understanding that some answer was expected from her, said a little tremulously, for she was hurt, "I cannot act a lie, Uncle Dinsmore, and poverty ought not to be considered a disgrace."

"Of course, it shouldn't, and I am not asking you to practice deceit any more than just to keep things to yourself which others have no right to pry into. It need not be difficult, for Mrs. Dinsmore is not one of the prying kind, and Horace and I will regard it as a favor to us, if you will simply leave it to me to take care of your expenses without question or remark."

This last was spoken with such winning kindness of tone and manner that even Mildred's pride was disarmed. Grateful tears shone in her eyes, as she turned them upon him.

"My dear, good uncle," she whispered, laying her

hand upon his with a gesture of confiding affection, "I don't know how to thank you and Cousin Horace, and I cannot refuse to do as you wish. But indeed, you must not let me be any more expense to you than if I were an ordinary guest, instead of the extraordinary one I am," she added, laughing to hide her emotion.

"I shall have my own way about it, you may depend, whatever that may chance to be," he answered with mock severity of tone.

Mildred laughed again, this time a really mirthful, happy laugh, feeling her heart grow strangely light.

After all, she could not help being glad that Mrs. Dinsmore was not to know their comparative poverty and that she herself was not to be looked upon as a poor relation who might be snubbed at pleasure and perhaps twitted with her lack of means, or worse still, treated with lofty—or with pitying— condescension.

"Yes," Mr. Dinsmore went on, half to himself, half to her, "wealth is but a secondary matter after all. Family is the main thing. I believe in blood and want nothing to do with the parvenu aristocracy, be they ever so rich. Well, what say you, my dear?" he asked, for Mildred's face had grown very thoughtful.

"I'm afraid I am naturally inclined to think just so, but—"

"Well, are not my views correct and proper?" he asked good humoredly, as she paused with a look of some confusion.

"Is not character what we should look at, rather than anything else?" she modestly inquired. "Is not true nobility that of the heart and life? It is what father and mother have taught me, and I think, too, it is most consistent with the teachings of God's Word."

At that moment, there was a sudden and large influx of passengers, some of them talking noisily, and her query went unanswered.

CHAPTER FIFTH

Walk boldly and wisely in that light thou hast.
There is a hand above will help thee on.

— BURLEY'S *FESTUS*

"WELL, MY DEAR, what do you think of her?" asked Mr. Dinsmore, addressing his wife.

Mildred had just left the room to don bonnet and shawl preparatory to a shopping expedition. She and her uncle had arrived in Philadelphia the previous night, and as Mrs. Dinsmore and the children had already retired, Mildred's first sight of them had been at the breakfast table this morning. Their meal was partaken of in the private parlor belonging to the suite of apartments the Dinsmores were occupying in one of the best hotels of the city.

"I am agreeably disappointed, I must confess," Mrs. Dinsmore replied to her husband's query. "She is decidedly pretty and extremely ladylike in manner and appearance. Even her dress—though not quite in fashion—shows her to be a person of taste and refinement. In fact, I think I shall enjoy playing chaperone to her and introducing her to our friends in the South."

"Ah, I thought you could not fail to be pleased with her," Mr. Dinsmore said, looking much gratified. "I knew you were when you bade her call you aunt. I imagine she had been a little troubled to decide just how she was to address you."

"Well, since I find she is not the sort one need feel ashamed of, I've no objection to her claiming relationship, though there is none at all in point of fact. But if she had proved the awkward, ungainly, uncouth girl I expected, I should have requested her to call me Mrs. Dinsmore," remarked that lady languidly. "I wonder if she has much shopping to do? I hope not, for I really do not feel equal to the exertion of assisting her."

"Driving about in a carriage and sitting in stores. I should not think it need be so very fatiguing," remarked her husband.

"Of course not, Mr. Dinsmore. Men never do see why anything should fatigue their wives," she retorted with some petulance.

"Then Miss Worth and I will have to manage it between us. You expect her today, do you not?"

"She was to come today, but of course she won't. People never do as they promise. The fact is, she oughtn't to have gone at all, leaving me here alone with servants and children. It was so selfish and inconsiderate!"

"But, my dear, it would have been very hard for her to go back without having spent a short time with her family."

"And her pleasure is to be considered before my comfort, of course."

"Really, I had hoped your comfort had not been at all neglected, my dear," Mr. Dinsmore said in a tone of some irritation as he glanced from the richly attired figure in the easy chair opposite his own to the luxurious appointments of the room. "What more could you wish?"

The entrance of Mrs. Dinsmore's maid, bringing her bonnet and shawl, saved the lady the necessity of replying to the somewhat inconvenient query, and her husband turned to the morning paper.

Then Mildred came in.

Mrs. Dinsmore, standing before the pier glass, saw the girl's figure reflected there, and the latter could not help enjoying her start of surprise.

"What an elegant shawl!" she exclaimed, turning hastily about to take a better view. "Real India! You needn't be ashamed to show yourself anywhere in that! Though your bonnet is quite out of date, as you warned me," she added by way of preventing too great an elation from her praise of the shawl.

"No matter about that," interposed Mr. Dinsmore, throwing down his paper. "We'll set that right. The carriage is waiting. Are any of the children going?"

"Yes, Adelaide, Louise, and Lora. Mammy and Fanny have taken the younger ones out."

The three little girls came in. They were expensively dressed in the height of fashion. They looked curiously at Mildred, and then Louise, the second in age and a child of ten, whispered to her mother, "What a frightful bonnet. It's not in the style at all, and I don't want her along if she's going to wear that."

"Hush! It's no matter," returned her mother in the same low key. "She won't be seen in the carriage, and we'll drive directly to Mrs. Brown's and get her a handsome one."

"Oh! What a pretty shawl, cousin," exclaimed Adelaide. "Real India, isn't it? Come on, mamma, and all of you," she added, hurrying into the hall. "it's time we were off."

"Adelaide always wants to direct the rest of us," complained Louise. "I wish, mamma, you'd make her know her place."

"Tut, tut! Remember, she's three years older than you. But if you children are going to quarrel, you must stay behind," said Mr. Dinsmore, standing back to let his wife and Mildred walk out first.

"No, no papa, that won't do, because we're to be fitted with hats and shoes," laughed the youngest of the three, putting her hand into his. "Besides, I didn't quarrel."

"That's true enough, Lora," he answered, leading her down the stairs. "In fact, I believe no one did but Louise, who is apt to be the complainer."

The drive to the milliner's was so short that Mildred thought they might as well have walked. She would have preferred it, giving her a better opportunity to see the city. But no, in that case she would have had to mortify her friends by a grand exhibition of her unfashionable headgear.

The next half hour was spent in turning over ribbons, flowers, and feathers, discussing styles, and trying on bonnets.

At length, one was found which pleased both Mrs.

Dinsmore and Mildred, but the price asked for it seemed to the latter extravagant.

"Do you think I ought to go so high, aunt?" she asked in an undertone. "Is it worth it?"

"I think the price reasonable and the hat no finer than you ought to wear," returned Mrs. Dinsmore coldly.

Mildred, blushing, turned to the saleswoman, saying, "I will take it," and began counting out the money to pay for it.

"Stay," said her aunt, "you will want a hat for traveling in."

A plainer and less expensive one was selected for that purpose. The handsome bonnet was put on, the bill paid, and they returned to their carriage, Mildred feeling pleasantly conscious of her improved appearance yet a trifle uneasy at the thought of how fast her money was melting away.

Their next visit was to a fashionable shoe store. Mrs. Dinsmore had the children and herself fitted with several pairs each, and by her advice, Mildred, too, bought slippers for the house and a pair of heavy walking shoes.

You must have, besides , a pair of gaiters to match each handsome dress you buy," Mrs. Dinsmore said to her as they re-entered the carriage.

That announcement filled Mildred with dismay. At this rate, her purse would be emptied before the demands upon it were nearly satisfied. What was she to do? She had been eager to select her dresses, but now she was thankful for the respite afforded her by Mrs. Dinsmore's declaration that she was too much fatigued for any more shopping and that they would return to their hotel.

"I'm going to lie down till it is time to dress for dinner and would advise you to do the same," she said to Mildred as they re-entered their parlor, and and our heroine retreated at once to her own room, glad of the opportunity to think over her perplexity in solitude. She would ask guidance and help of her best Friend, who, as she rejoiced in knowing, was abundantly able and willing to help her in every time of need.

She cast her burden on Him, then threw herself on the bed. Being very weary from her long journey, she soon fell asleep.

Two hours later, she was roused by a knock at her door. She sprang up and opened it to find a porter there with an armful of brown paper parcels and a note for her.

"Is there not some mistake?" she asked in surprise.

"No, Miss, No. 95, and here's the name on the note and the bundles."

"Why, yes, it is my name, sure enough!" she exclaimed. "Well, you may bring them in."

The man laid the packages down and departed, while Mildred, only waiting to close the door on him, tore open the note.

My dear niece,

You must please excuse the liberty I have taken in selecting your dresses for you. Your Aunt Wealthy put some money into my hands to be laid out for you. The letter, containing her remittance and also one from Roselands that hurries us home, came to hand a few minutes after you and Mrs. Dinsmore had left the hotel. Miss Worth arrived while I was in the act of reading them, and with her assistance, I ventured to do your shopping for you. The contents of the parcels sent with this are the result.

Hoping they may suit your taste, I am ever your affectionate uncle, A.D.

For some minutes after the note had been hastily read and laid aside, Mildred's fingers were very busy with twine and wrapping paper, bringing to light beautiful and costly things, while her cheeks burned with excitement and her eyes danced with delight or filled with tears of mingled pleasure and pain.

She could not fail to rejoice in such a wealth of lovely things, yet it hurt her pride of independence that she must take them as gifts—and from one who was scarcely related to her, for well she knew that Mr. Dinsmore must have paid a large proportion of the price from his own purse.

There were materials for three beautiful evening dresses, a sage-colored merino very fine and soft, an all-wool delaine in a royal purple with an embroidered sprig. There were also three silks—a black, a dark brown, and a silver gray, each rich and heavy enough to almost stand alone. There was a box of kid gloves—one or two pairs to match each dress and the rest white for evening wear. Nor had suitable trimmings for the dresses been forgotten. They were there in beautiful variety—ribbons, buttons, heavy silk fringes. Nothing had been overlooked.

Mildred seemed to be in a dream. She could hardly believe that such riches were really here.

There came a rap at the door, and opening it, she found Mr. Dinsmore standing there.

"May I come in?" he asked with grave cheerfulness.

She stepped back silently, her heart too full for speech. Entering, he closed the door.

"My dear child, you will kindly excuse me?" he began, but Mildred threw her arms round his neck and burst into tears.

"Oh, uncle, you are so kind! But it is too much," she sobbed, hiding her face on his shoulder.

"Nonsense! The merest trifle!" he said, stroking her hair. "But if you don't like them—"

"Like them!" she cried. "They're just lovely! Every one of them, but—"

"No, no! No buts," he said cheerily. "If they suit your taste, it's all right. The gaiters that Mrs. Dinsmore says are necessary to match the dresses can be made to match the dresses and can be made nearer home. We'll have two days, Friday and Saturday, for sightseeing. This is Thursday, and early Monday morning we leave for Roselands."

"But, oh, uncle, you shouldn't have spent so much money on me," began Mildred.

"I, child? Your Aunt Wealthy, you mean. Didn't you read my note?"

"Yes, sir, and I know I must thank her for a part, but only a part, of these beautiful things."

"Dear me, how very wise you are," he said jokingly, chucking her playfully under her chin. "Yet perhaps not quite so wise as we think. Now, if you want to do me a favor, just call to mind our talk in the cars the other day and say no more about this.

"Mrs. Dinsmore and Miss Worth know nothing but that I had money of yours in my hands and have used it in doing your shopping for you. It is decidedly my wish that they neither know nor suspect anything further. Will you oblige me by being quiet about it?"

"I would do anything I possibly could to oblige you, Uncle Dinsmore," she answered, looking into his eyes with hers full of grateful tears.

"Ah, that's my good girl," he said. "Now dry your eyes, and we'll go down to dinner. It's to be served for the family in our own parlor, and it is probably on the table now."

Dinner was on the table, and as they entered, the family were in the act of taking their places about it.

Miss Worth, the governess, was with them. She was an intelligent-looking but rather plain-featured woman of perhaps thirty-five. Her manners were unobtrusive and she was very quiet and reserved, seemingly self-absorbed.

Mildred's first impressions were not too favorable. The thought in the girl's mind was: "She's a disagreeable old maid, and I'm sure I shall never like her."

Yet the face, though slightly sad and careworn when at rest, would by many have been preferred to Mrs. Dinsmore's in its faded beauty and listless or fretful and annoyed expression.

The bright, fresh young faces of the children pleased Mildred better than either. There were six of them in all. Arthur, Walter, and Enna were all younger than the three little girls whose acquaintance she had made in the morning. The last named was a mere baby. They were pretty children and not ill-behaved considering that they had been used to an almost unlimited amount of indulgence.

"Miss Worth has been telling me about the dresses, Mildred," remarked Mrs. Dinsmore. "I hope you will like them. I should think from her description, they must be very handsome."

"They are, *very*," Mildred answered with a vivid blush. "I don't think I could possibly have been better suited." Turning to Miss Worth, she thanked her warmly for the trouble she had taken on her behalf.

"It was no trouble, and you are heartily welcome, Miss Keith," returned the governess, a smile lighting up her features into positive comeliness.

Mr. Dinsmore changed the subject by a kind proposal to take his wife and Mildred to some place of amusement for the evening.

"How thoughtless you are, my dear," said Mrs. Dinsmore. "I am sure Mildred must be too much fatigued by her journey to think of going out."

"I doubt it," he returned laughingly. "What do you say, Milly?"

"That I don't think I am," she answered brightly. "A two-hour nap this afternoon has refreshed me quite wonderfully."

"Then we'll go," he said. "There's an opportunity to hear some fine music, and I don't want to miss it. You will go with us, Mrs. Dinsmore?"

"No," she said coldly. "I do not feel equal to the exertion."

She was not an invalid but had barely escaped becoming such through extreme aversion to exercise of body or mind.

Mr. Dinsmore then extended his invitation to Miss Worth, overruled her objection that she feared the children would require her attention by saying that the servants would give them all the care they needed, and insisted upon her acceptance, unless she, too, must plead fatigue as an excuse for declining.

Before the governess had time to open her lips in reply, Mrs. Dinsmore suddenly announced that she had changed her mind. She would go, she said, and she went on to say that she could not feel easy about the children unless Miss Worth were there to see that they were properly attended to.

It was a disappointment to the latter, who seldom enjoyed such a treat, but she quietly acquiesced, sighing inwardly but giving no outward sign.

"Shall we walk or ride?" asked Mr. Dinsmore, looking at Mildred. "The distance is about four squares."

"Oh, let us walk," she was about to exclaim, feeling an eager desire for the exercise and to look at the buildings and brightly lighted windows, but Mrs. Dinsmore decided this question also with an emphatic, "We will take the carriage, of course. What can you be thinking of, Mr. Dinsmore?"

They had left the table., and Mildred was considering how she should excuse herself so that she might retire to her own room and finish a letter to her mother when Mrs. Dinsmore said, "You must show me your pretty things now, Mildred. There'll be plenty of time before we have to dress for the concert."

"Dress!" echoed Mildred in dismay. "Really, Aunt, I have nothing more suitable than this I have on," glancing down at the blue-black silk she had been wearing all day.

"What does it matter? That's neat fitting and handsome enough for any occasion," interrupted Mr. Dinsmore.

"It will do very well, if you don't throw back your shawl," remarked his wife, glancing askance at the neat, ladylike, and pretty dress.

"The place will be crowded and warm," said Mr. Dinsmore. "If you find your shawl burdensome, Mildred, you are to throw it back and be comfortable." His wife gave him an indignant glance.

"She can take a fan," she said shortly. "I'll lend her one that I'll not be ashamed to see her carry."

Mildred was glad she could say she had a pretty fan of her own and would not need to borrow one. With it, she said, she would doubtless be able to refrain from throwing back her shawl in a way to exhibit the unfashionable make of her dress.

Mrs. Dinsmore graciously condescended to approve of the purchases made by her husband and the governess, saying she really thought she hardly could have done better herself, and it was an immense relief to know that the thing was done without any worry or responsibility coming upon her, she being so ill able to bear such things.

On hearing this information, Mildred felt quite thankful that her assistance had not been asked.

Mildred enjoyed the concert extremely, and the sightseeing, which with a little more shopping, fully occupied the next two days, and the church-going of the day following. She found time before breakfast Saturday morning to do her packing and to finish the letter to her mother. On Monday morning, there was little time for anything but breakfast before they must go on board the steamer which was to carry them to the seaport town within a few miles of Roselands.

CHAPTER SIXTH

O'er the glad waters of the dark, blue sea.

— BYRON

IT WAS MILDRED'S first sight of the ocean. The November air had a chill, but the sun shone brightly. Well wrapped up, she found the deck not an uncomfortable place, so she kept her station there all through the passage down the river and bay, though Mrs. Dinsmore very soon retreated, shivering, to the cabin. She called in nurses and children, with the exception of Adelaide, who insisted upon remaining with her father and cousin and was, as usual, allowed to have her own way.

"There, we have a full view of old ocean," Mr. Dinsmore said, as they steamed out of the bay. "You never saw anything like that before, Mildred?"

"Yes, the Great Lakes look very similar, I think," she answered, gazing away over the restless waters, her eyes kindling with enthusiasm. "How grandly beautiful it is! I think I should never weary of the sight, and I should like to live where I could watch it day by day in all its moods."

"Roselands is not so very far from the coast,"

said Adelaide. "A ride of a few miles in one direction gives us a distant view."

"Oh, I am glad of that!" Mildred exclaimed.

"And we will place a pony and a servant at your command, so that you can ride in that direction whenever you will," added Mr. Dinsmore.

Mildred took her eyes from the sea long enough to give him a look of delight that fully repaid him. Nor did she spare words but told him he was wonderfully kind to her.

"Tell about being on the lakes, cousin," pleaded Adelaide. "When was it, and who was with you?"

There had been a little homesickness tugging at Mildred's heartstrings, and that last question brought tears to her eyes and a tremble to her lips. She had a short struggle with herself before she could so command her voice as to speak quite steadily.

But when she had once begun, it was not difficult to go on and give a circumstantial account of their journey to Indiana, especially as Adelaide proved a delighted and deeply interested listener.

"Thank you," she said, when the story had come to an end. "But do tell me more about your brothers and sisters—everything you can think of. What a lot of them there are! I think Cyril and Don must be comical little fellows."

"Yes, and very provokingly mischievous at times," Mildred said, laughing at the recollection of some of their pranks, which she went on to describe for Adelaide's entertainment.

But the sun had set, and the air was so cold that they were compelled to seek the shelter of the cabin.

They found warmth and brightness there. Mrs. Dinsmore was half reclining on a sofa, her husband reading the evening paper by her side.

"Well, I'm glad you've come in at last," she said with a reproachful look directed at Mildred. "It was really very thoughtless to keep Adelaide out so late."

"She didn't keep me, mamma," answered the child with spirit. "I could have come in any minute if I had chosen. I was not even asked to stay."

"Don't be pert, Adelaide," said her mother. "Dear me, how the vessel begins to rock! I shall be deathly sick before morning."

"That would have been less likely to happen if you had followed Mildred's example in staying on the deck as long as possible," remarked her husband, turning his paper and beginning another article.

"I should have caught my death of cold," she retorted snappishly, "but perhaps you wouldn't have cared if I had. And I think it's quite insulting to have a child like that held up to me as an example."

Mildred had walked away and did not here the last remark. Adelaide had slipped her hand into Mildred's and was saying, "I like you, cousin. We'll be good friends, shan't we?"

"It shall not be my fault if we're not," Mildred said, forcing a smile. Mrs. Dinsmore's fault-finding had hurt her feelings and caused a decided increase of the homesickness. But determined to overcome it, she gathered the children about her at a safe distance from their mother and told them some stories till interrupted by the summons to the tea table.

They had a rather rough sea that night and the next day, causing a good deal of sickness among the passengers. Mildred, taught by past experience, fought bravely against it by seeking the deck soon after sunrise and spending almost the whole day there in company with her uncle.

The second day she experienced no difficulty and was joined by her cousins. But Mrs. Dinsmore kept to her berth till the end of the voyage, and when the vessel arrived in port, she came from her stateroom pale, weak, and disconsolate.

The last stage of the journey was made in carriages.

They reached Roselands just as the sun was setting amid a mass of crimson, gold, and amber-colored clouds forming a gorgeous background to a landscape of more than ordinary beauty.

"Oh, how lovely!" exclaimed Mildred as her uncle handed her from the carriage. "I was prepared to be charmed by the place, but it exceeds my expectations."

"Let me bid you welcome and hope that first impressions may prove lasting and your stay here most enjoyable," he said with a gratified smile.

But now Mildred's attention was attracted to the reception that had been prepared for them — just such a one as she had often heard described by her mother.

The plantation was large, the dwelling also. A dozen or more of the house servants, headed by the housekeeper, had ranged themselves in a double row across the veranda and down the wide entrance hall.

Their faces were full of delight, and their hands held out in joyous greeting with glad words of welcome on every tongue, as master, mistress, guest, and children and their attendants passed slowly between the ranks, shaking hands and making kind inquiries right and left.

Some of the older ones remembered Mildred's mother, and our heroine's heart warmed toward them as they sounded "Miss Marcia's" praises and averred that her daughter bore a striking resemblance to her in looks.

"Mrs. Brown, this young lady is my niece," said Mr. Dinsmore, laying a hand on Mildred's shoulder and addressing himself to the housekeeper, "and I commend her to your special care. Please see that she is well waited upon and wants for nothing that house or plantation can supply. Here, Rachel," he said to a young servant girl, "I appoint you Miss Mildred's waiting maid. You are to be always at her call and do whatever she directs."

"Yes, massa," the girl answered, dropping a deep curtsy, first to him, then to Mildred, whom she regarded with a look of smiling approval. "Dis chile berry glad ob de chance. Shall I show de way to yo' room, now, miss?" Mildred gave a smiling assent, and she was immediately conducted to a spacious, elegantly furnished apartment, where an open wood fire blazed and crackled, sending around a ruddy light that rendered that of the wax candles in the heavy, polished-silver candlesticks on the mantel almost superfluous.

Mildred sent a very satisfied, appreciative glance about her. Then, turning to her young handmaiden, who stood quietly awaiting her orders, she asked if there were time to change her dress before tea.

"Yes, Miss, plenty o' time. Whar yo' trunks, Miss? Oh! Heyah dey come," she said, slipping out of the way of two of the men servants as they entered with Mildred's luggage.

Mrs. Brown followed close in their rear, bade them unstrap the trunks before leaving, inquired of Mildred if there were anything more she could do for her, and said she hoped she would be very comfortable.

"Rachel is young and has not had much experience in the duties of a ladies' maid," she added, "but I think you will find her trusty and willing. Would you not like to have her unpack your things and arrange them in the bureau and wardrobe? Then the trunks can be put away out of sight till they are wanted again later."

"Yes, that will be nice," said Mildred, producing the keys. "But will there be time before tea?"

"Hardly, I'm afraid, Miss Keith, if you have any change to make in your dress. But you should have time later in the evening, if that will answer?"

"Oh, yes, quite as well."

Mrs. Brown took her departure. Mr. Dinsmore looked in for a moment to see that his young guest had not been neglected and how she was pleased with her new quarters. Then Mildred, left alone with her maid, opened a trunk, laid out the dress and ornaments she wished to wear, and proceeded, with Rachel's assistance, to make her somewhat hurried preparations for tea.

The tea bell rang, and Adelaide's bright face peeped in at the door.

"Ready, cousin? I'll show you the way."

They entered the dining room looking fresh and blooming as two roses.

Mr. Dinsmore assigned Mildred the seat of honor at his right hand and complimented her on the becomingness of her attire.

She was the only guest, the children were all allowed to come to the table, and they were a merry family party, everybody rejoicing in being at home again after an absence of several months.

The table was loaded with delicacies, skillfully prepared, for Old Phoebe, the cook, was a real genius in the culinary art. The cloth was of a finest damask, the service of rare china and costly silver-ware, and the attendance all that could be desired.

Pleading excessive fatigue from the journey, Mrs. Dinsmore retired to her own apartments immediately upon the conclusion of the meal.

"You look quite too fresh and bright to be thinking of bed yet," Mr. Dinsmore remarked, laying his hand affectionately on Mildred's shoulder. "Will you come to the library with me?"

She gave a pleased assent, and they were soon cozily seated on either side of the fire there. A table covered with books, papers, and periodicals was drawn up between them.

"How do you like this room, Milly?" Mr. Dinsmore asked.

"Oh, very much!" Mildred answered, sending a sweeping glance from side to side and noting all the attractions of the place, from the rich Turkish carpet, handsome rugs, comfortable chairs, couches, and tables to the long lines of well-filled bookshelves, statues, statuettes and busts, and two or three fine paintings on the walls.

"That is right," he said with a pleased smile. "I want you to feel perfectly at home here, coming in whenever you please and staying just as long as you like, reading, writing, studying, or lounging. Help yourself with perfect freedom to books and writing materials, for whatever is in the room is entirely at your service."

Mildred was beginning to thank him, but he cut her short. "Never mind that. Here's far better occupation for you," he said, handing her a package of letters as he spoke.

She took it with a joyful exclamation. "Letters from home! Oh, I have been so hungry for them."

"Yes," he said, enjoying her delight, "but don't run away," he added, for she had risen to her feet, evidently with that intention. "Perhaps there may be a bit here and there you'd like to read to me. If they bring tears to your eyes, I'll not think the worse of you. Besides, I shall be too busy with my own correspondence to take notice."

So she sat down again and presently forgot his presence in the interest of those written pages that seemed almost to transport her into the very midst of the dear home circle.

It was a family letter, everyone from her father down to Annis contributing something. The little ones had each dictated a message to "Sister Milly," but the greater part was from her mother, giving in pleasing detail the doings, sayings, and plannings in their little world, the small successes and failures, the apparently trivial occurrences, the little joys and sorrows, little trials and vexations, and the little pleasures that make or mar the happiness of daily home life.

The mother's sweet, loving, trustful spirit breathed through it all. There were little jests that brought a smile to Mildred's lips or made her laugh outright — and these she read aloud to her uncle. There were words of faith and patience that filled her eyes with tears, and at the last, tender, motherly counsels that stirred her heart to its inmost depths.

She would have given a great deal at that moment to be at home again within sound of that beloved voice, looking into the dear eyes and feeling the gentle touch of the soft, caressing hand. Oh, could she stay away for months?

The tears would come. She rose, crossed the room, and stood before a painting with her back to her uncle, who at that instant seemed wholly absorbed in a business letter he held in his hand.

Recovering herself, she came back to the table.

Mr. Dinsmore looked up.

"I think we must have a ride tomorrow morning, Milly, you and Adelaide and I. Shall it be at nine o'clock?"

Her eyes grew bright, and her cheeks flushed with pleasure. She was very fond of riding on horseback.

"I shall be delighted to go, uncle," she said, "and I can be ready at any hour that may suit you best."

He considered a moment.

"I should not be surprised if you and Adie find yourselves inclined to take a long morning nap after your journey," he said. "We will say directly after breakfast, which will not be earlier than nine. Now I see you want to retire, so bid me goodnight and away with you to slumbers sweet." And with a fatherly kiss, he dismissed her.

Mildred's room was as bright, warm, and cheery as she had left it. Rachel was not there, and the trunks had vanished also. But the opening of wardrobe doors and bureau drawers showed their contents neatly stowed therein.

An easy chair stood invitingly before the fire, and dropping into it, Mildred gave her letter a second perusal, mingling laughter and tears over it as before.

She sighed softly to herself as she folded it up. Glancing about the spacious, handsomely appointed room, she smiled at the thought of the contrast between her present surroundings and those of a few weeks ago, when she was occupying a small, very plainly furnished room and, instead of having a maid at her beck and call, was constantly waiting upon and working for others.

The rest and ease of the present were certainly very enjoyable, yet she had no desire that the change should become a permanent one. Home, with all its toils and cares, was still the sweetest, dearest place on earth to her.

Rachel came in to replenish the fire and ask if there was anything more she could do for the young lady's comfort.

"No, thank you, my wants are fully supplied," Mildred said with a smile. "I think I shall get ready for bed now."

"Den missy want her slippers and night clo's," remarked the girl, hastening to bring them. "Shall dis chile take down yo' hair and brush um out?"

"Yes," Mildred said. "When I have put on my dressing gown. And I'll read to you while you do it."

"Tank you, missy, dis chile be berry glad to hear readin'," the girl answered with a look of pleasure. "She can't read none herself and neber expects to know how."

"Then I'll read the Bible to you every night and morning while you do up my hair," Mildred said. "It is God's word, Rachel, His letter to tell us the way to heaven, and we all need to know what it says."

"'Spect we does, miss," responded the girl with wide-open, wondering eyes fixed on Mildred's face. "But nobody neber tole me dat befo'."

"Then here is work for me to do for the Master," thought Mildred, and she sent up a silent petition, "Lord, teach me how to lead her to Thee."

CHAPTER SEVENTH

O thou child of many prayers!
Life hath quicksands, life hath snares!

—LONGFELLOW

A BRIGHT RAY OF sunshine stealing in between the silken curtains fell across Mildred's eyes and awakened her.

The fire was blazing cheerily on the hearth. Rachel was at hand to wait upon her, and she found it by no means unpleasant to sit still and have her hair skillfully arranged for her instead of doing the work with her own hands, as she had been accustomed to do since she was quite a little girl.

She occupied herself the while in reading aloud from the Bible, according to her promise, and Rachel seemed well pleased to listen.

Her dressing completed, Mildred went to the library to answer her letter while waiting for the breakfast bell, and there Mr. Dinsmore found her.

"That is quite right," he said. "Send my love to them all, but don't close your letter yet. You'll want to tell your mother about your ride. We'll take one that used to be a favorite with her."

Mildred looked up brightly. "I shall enjoy it all the more for knowing that."

"You are accustomed to riding on horseback?" he said inquiringly.

"Enough to be able to keep my seat on a well-behaved steed," she answered laughingly. "I hope to improve very much under your instruction, Uncle Dismore."

"Gyp, the pony I have assigned to you while you stay, is quite safe, I think, sufficiently spirited but well trained," he said, giving her his arm to conduct her into the breakfast room, for the bell had just rung.

"I hear you are going to ride, Mildred," Mrs. Dinsmore remarked, as they rose from the table. "Have you a riding habit?"

Mildred was very glad to be able to answer in the affirmative.

The horses were already at the door.

She hurried to her room and was down in a few minutes arrayed in a manner that entirely satisfied Mrs. Dinsmore.

It was a delicious morning. Riders and steeds seemed alike in fine spirits, and Mildred had seldom found anything more enjoyable than the brisk canter of the next hour over a good road and through new and pleasing scenes.

On their return, Mrs. Dinsmore followed her to her room.

"You must have some of your dresses made at once, Mildred," she said. "Can you get out the materials and come now to the sewing room to be fitted? The black silk should be first, I think, and finished this week, so that you may have it to wear to church next Sunday."

"You are very kind," Mildred said, looking much pleased. "But are not the services of your seamstresses needed just now for yourself and the children?"

"No, there is nothing hurrying," was the reply. "We all had fall dresses made up in Philadelphia, and you must be prepared to show yourself to visitors, for our friends and neighbors will soon be calling on you, as well as on us. Of course, I shall take pride in having them find my husband's niece suitably attired."

Mildred was loath to decline the offer. In fact, she was filled with an eager desire, natural to her age, to see how all these beautiful things would look when all made up and how well they would become her.

But her love of independence and the industrious habits in which she had been trained alike forbade her to leave all the work to Mrs. Dinsmore's maids. Her own deft and busy fingers accomplished no small share of it, the greater part of every day for the next two or three weeks being occupied in that way.

Mrs. Dinsmore disliked exertion of any kind and seldom took a needle in her hand, but she had no distaste toward seeing others so employed. She generally spent her mornings lounging in the sewing room, ready to give her opinion in regard to the style of trimming and so forth, and enjoying a comfortable sense of conferring a great favor thereby.

The black silk was completed in time to be worn on Mildred's first Sunday at Roselands, and Mrs. Dinsmore, subjecting her to careful scrutiny when she came down dressed for church, assured her that she was quite a stylish-looking young lady whom she herself was not ashamed to exhibit to her acquaintances as belonging to the Dinsmore family.

A glance into a pier glass in the drawing room told Mildred the compliment was not undeserved, and I fear there was no little gratified vanity in the smile with which she turned away and followed her aunt to the carriage waiting for them at the door. I also fear the consciousness of her finery and its becomingness seriously interfered with the heartiness of her devotions in the house of God and the attention she should have given to the preaching of the Word and the services of prayer and praise.

She was in some measure aware of this herself, and she felt condemned on account of it. But she was not helped to recover lost ground by the worldly conversation carried on about her during much of the day.

There was a good deal of friendly chat in the vestibule of the church after the close of the services, neighbors and acquaintances gathering about the Dinsmores to welcome and congratulate them on their return from their late trip and inquire concerning their health and enjoyment of their lengthened sojourn in the North.

Mr. Dinsmore was extremely hospitable and fond of entertaining his friends, nor had he any scruples about doing so on the Sabbath. At his urgent invitation, two gentlemen and a brightly dressed and lively young lady accompanied his family and himself to Roselands to dine and spend the remainder of the day.

The talk was just what it might have been on any other occasion—of politics, amusements, dress, and anything and everything but the topics suited to the sacredness of the day. And Mildred, while yielding to the temptation to join in, felt painfully conscious that in so doing she was not obeying the command, "Remember the Sabbath day to keep it holy."

It was late in the evening when the visitors had left, and she returned to her room weary and sleepy. She hurried through the form of devotion, giving but little heart to it, and was soon in bed and asleep.

She tried to do better the next morning, but her thoughts ran very much to dress and the vanities.

"How could I help that?" she asked herself, half despairingly, half in excuse. "I must assist in making my clothes and decide, too, how it should be done."

Another dress was begun that day, and her head and hands were fully occupied over it.

Her uncle insisted on a ride or walk every day, callers began to come, and hours had to be spent in the drawing room. Work on the dresses had to be pushed all the harder the rest of the day to recover lost time.

Then she must attire herself in her most becoming finery and drive out with Mrs. Dinsmore to return the calls, during which the talk generally ran upon the merest trifles, furnishing no food for mind or heart.

Flatteries and compliments were showered upon our heroine, for she was pretty, graceful, and refined. She was quick at repartee, self-possessed without being conceited, well informed for her years, and a good conversationalist.

Her aunt and uncle were altogether satisfied with the impression she made, but her parents would have been sorely troubled could they have known how the world and its vanities were engrossing the thoughts of their beloved child to the exclusion of better things.

There were brilliant entertainments given in her honor—first by Mrs. Dinsmore and afterward by others who had been her invited guests.

The weather continuing remarkably mild and pleasant for some weeks, there were excursions gotten up to various points of interest in the vicinity. There were dinner parties and tea drinkings and days when the house was filled with merry company from morning to night. Sometimes, Mr. and Mrs. Dinsmore visited in a like manner at the houses of neighboring planters, taking Mildred with them.

Then there were the drives to the city: in the daytime to shop for more finery, in the evening for the purpose of attending some place of amusement—now a concert, now a lecture, and later the opera and the theater.

In these latter and questionable, not to say even forbidden, places of resort to one reared as Mildred had been, she was at first decoyed. But becoming intoxicated with their sensual sweets, she went again and again of her own free will.

Thus, for a month or more, she ran a giddy round of worldly pleasures, scarcely taking time to think and refusing to listen to the warnings and the upbraidings of her conscience.

But her merry-making began to tell unfavorably upon her health, the recovery of which had been her principal object in leaving home, and she was obliged to relinquish them in part.

Then a long storm set in, confining her to the house for a week and keeping away visitors. She was forced to stop and consider, and a long, loving letter from her mother coming just then, freighted with words of Christian counsel, had a blessed effect in helping to open her eyes to her guilt and danger.

In the silence and solitude of her room, with the sighing of the wind outside and the rain and sleet beating against the windows the only sounds reaching her ears, Mildred read and wept over this letter and over the mental review of the life she had been leading since coming to Róselands.

To one more worldly, it might have seemed innocent enough, but it was not so to Mildred's enlightened conscience. A butterfly existence was not the end for which she had been created, yet she could not shut her eyes to the fact that that was the best that could be said of her life of late. She had been neither doing nor getting any good but rather the contrary. She was injuring her health by her dissipations, setting an example of worldliness, and falling behind in the Christian race.

She had not neglected the forms of religious service. She had attended church every Sunday, read her Bible, and repeated a prayer night and morning. But all her thoughts, as she now saw with grief and shame, with a sadly wandering heart, had been full of dress and earthly vanities.

Alas, how far she had wandered out of the way in which she had covenanted to walk! And that, though she had proved in days past that "wisdom's ways were ways of pleasantness, and all her paths were peace."

And as she questioned whether she had found real enjoyment in these bypaths of worldliness, she was forced to acknowledge that in spite of much thoughtless gaiety and mirth, there had been no genuine, solid happiness. Instead, there was a secret uneasiness which she vainly strove to banish and could only forget for a time in the giddy round of amusement.

Should she go on as she had begun? No. By the help of God she would turn and find again the path she had left, even as her mother in this timely letter advised and entreated.

Mrs. Keith knew to some extent the worldly atmosphere of the house into which her young daughter had gone, and she had written with the fear in her heart that Mildred might succumb to its temptations even as she had done.

She entreated her to be on her guard, watching unto prayer and thus keeping close to the Master.

"And, dear daughter," she added, "should you ever find that you have wandered, lose not a moment in returning to Him and pleading for cleansing, for pardon, and for restoration through His own precious blood. Let not Satan tempt you to stay away one moment with the lie that the Lord is not ever waiting to be gracious and ever ready and willing to forgive, or that He would have you delay till your repentance is deeper or you have done something to atone in some measure for your sin.

"God's time is always now to the backslider in heart or life, as well as to the impenitent sinner. To both, He says, 'Him that cometh unto Me, I will in no wise cast out!'"

CHAPTER EIGHTH

*I have deeply felt
The mockery of the hollow shrine at
which my spirit knelt.*

—WHITTIER

MILDRED HAD BEEN alone for several hours—very profitable ones for her—when opening the door in answer to a gentle rap, she found Mr. Dinsmore standing there.

"If you will invite me in," he said with a smile, "I may perhaps accept."

"Do come in, uncle," she replied, returning the smile. "It is very pleasant here, and I can give you a warm welcome. See, my fire is blazing cheerily, and does not that easy chair look inviting?"

"Yes," he answered, taking her hand and gazing searchingly into her face, seeing something there that puzzled him greatly. For though the traces of tears were very evident, it wore a look of peace that had been foreign to it of late. "But whatever is the matter? Not bad news from home, I hope."

"No, oh no!" she said. "They were all well and nothing was amiss when mother wrote." But her eyes filled, and her lips quivered as she spoke.

"Homesick, I'm afraid," he said kindly, patting and stroking the hand he held. "It is the natural effect of news from there, I suppose, especially in this wretched weather. But don't give up to it, my dear. We'll find ways to make the time pass pleasantly in spite of the storm—home sports, amusing books."

"You are very kind always, dear uncle," she said with a grateful look, "but it is not that. I have been living too much for mere amusement of late."

And with burning cheeks and tear-dimmed eyes, she went on to explain in a few rapid sentences how condemned she felt on account of the waste of time and opportunities for improvement, and the worldly conformity of which she had been guilty, and how she had determined, by God's help, to do so no more.

He listened in much surprise but did not interrupt her.

When she had finished, there was a moment's silence, she sitting with downcast eyes, her breast still heaving with emotion, and he gazing musingly into the fire.

Presently, he turned to look at her again with a kindly smile.

"Thank you, my dear, for your confidence," he said pleasantly. "But really, I do not see that you have done anything to be distressed about. It strikes me that you were fairly entitled to a few weeks of playtime after the fatigues of that long nursing and the journey here."

"Perhaps so," she said, "but I haven't taken just the right sort. So much excitement and such late hours have wearied instead of rested me physically, and on my spiritual nature the effect has been still worse. I blame no one but myself," she added humbly and with a deprecating look into his grave, somewhat troubled face.

"I'm afraid I have been your tempter," he said, "though I meant well. But I ought to have remembered the strict ideas entertained by your parents and in which they have brought you up. Well, what can I do to retrieve my error and to help you in living as you think you should?"

"It mostly depends upon myself, I think," she answered thoughtfully. "But if you will not oppose me in declining invitations to what I deem wrong or questionable amusements, and will excuse me from attendance in the drawing room on Sundays when there is company, it will help me very much."

"My dear girl," he returned, "you are of course perfectly free to do exactly as you please in both respects. We appreciate your society, but if you think it best to withdraw it from us, we can only submit. I will arrange with Mrs. Dinsmore that young people shall be invited on weekdays and only older people, whom you will not feel called upon to entertain, on Sundays."

She thanked him warmly.

"And you will give up the opera and theater?" he said inquiringly. "I thought you had enjoyed them very much."

"I did," she answered, blushing.

"Then why resign so innocent a pleasure?"

"It is not innocent for me, uncle," she said, lifting her glistening eyes to his. "It utterly destroys the spirit of devotion. I come from them with my mind full of the play and thoughts about dress and the merry people I have seen and with no heart for prayer or the study of God's word. The short-lived pleasure I derive from them is nothing to be compared with the sweet peace and joy they rob me of."

"But if you persist in such a course of conduct, you will be sneered at as self-righteous, puritanical, and whatnot—politely to your face, more disagreeably behind your back."

"I am willing to be singular for Christ," she answered, her eyes kindling. "Oh, how little that would be to bear for Him compared with what He endured for me! How much less I resign than multitudes of others have given up for Him! Moses chose 'rather to suffer affliction with the people of God, than to enjoy the pleasures of sin for a season, esteeming the reproach of Christ greater riches than the treasures of Egypt.'"

"And you purpose to begin doing something in the way of study and the cultivation of your accomplishments?" he said inquiringly, not unwilling to change the subject of conversation.

"Yes, uncle, I should like to accept your generous offer to let me share in the instruction of Adelaide's masters in music, painting, French, and German, and Miss Worth's in the higher mathematics."

"All that will keep you pretty busy even without the reading you are sure to do," he commented with a smile.

"Usefully employed," she answered brightly, "and that, I have learned from experience, is the way to be happy."

The first sneer Mildred had to bear came from Mrs. Dinsmore, who heard with great vexation her husband's report of the young girl's resolve.

"Ridiculous!" she exclaimed. "If there's anything I do detest and despise, it is your rigid, puritanical sectary, who stands ready to cry out 'sinful! wicked!' at every sort of enjoyment! I am too much provoked. She is really a pretty and ladylike girl, and she has attracted a good deal of attention, so that I was actually growing quite proud of her and took pleasure in showing her off.

"But that is all over now, of course, and there'll be no end to the annoyance I shall have to endure in hearing her criticized for her odd behavior and in parrying questions and remarks as to how she came by such strange notions."

"Well, my dear, it can't be helped," Mr. Dinsmore responded between a smile and a sigh. If I were you, I should decidedly snub anyone who should offer one disparaging remark about her to me. Being myself, I certainly intend to do so."

"Can't be helped! I believe you could reason her out of it if you would!"

"I am flattered by your belief but do not share it," he said with a bow of acknowledgment. "Nor if I did, would I attempt to change her views. 'Twould be too great a responsibility and a breach of the trust her parents have reposed in me."

The conversation was here brought to a conclusion by the summons to the dinner table.

Mildred made her appearance with the rest and was greeted by Mrs. Dinsmore with a cold inquiry after her health, followed by a covert taunt in regard to her resolve to forsake the worldly amusements in which she had of late indulged.

Mildred bore it with patience and humility, "not answering again," though the flushing of her cheek showed that she felt the unkindness keenly enough.

"Do you intend to make a complete hermit of yourself and go nowhere at all?" queried the irate lady.

"Oh, no, aunt," returned Mildred pleasantly. "I hope still to take walks, rides, and drives, and I do not object to calls and social visits or to concerts or lectures, unless attending necessitates the keeping of later hours than are good for my health."

"Humph! 'Twould have been wiser, to my thinking, if you had begun as you meant to continue."

"Yes, auntie, it would have been," Mildred said, again coloring deeply. "I wish I had, but it is better to do right at last than not at all. Do you not think so?"

"Don't ask me," she replied sharply. "Adelaide, Louise, and Lora, you may consider yourselves fortunate in having a cousin who is more capable of deciding questions of duty than your parents. I trust you will not fail to profit by her excellent example — not that which she has set, you will observe, but that which she is going to set for you in the future."

The children giggled, while Mildred colored more deeply than before.

A frown had gathered on Mr. Dinsmore's brow.

"Children, if you cannot behave properly, you must leave the table," he said sternly. Then with a displeased look at his wife, he continued, "I, for one, highly approve of Mildred's resolve to do what she considers her duty, and it is my desire that she be allowed to follow the dictates of her conscience in peace."

Mr. Dinsmore was an indulgent husband and seldom found fault with anything his wife chose to do or say, but experience had taught her that when he did interfere, she had better submit at once. The subject was dropped and never revived again in his presence.

With her accustomed promptness and energy, Mildred sought out Miss Worth that very afternoon, made arrangements for recitations, and began her studies in earnest.

She determined to devote four hours a day to them and her accomplishments. As she was accustomed to early rising and the breakfast hour at Roselands was late, it would not be difficult, she thought, to secure two hours before that meal. The other two she would take during Mrs. Dinsmore's afternoon siesta and the elaborate dressing which usually followed. Thus, she would be as much as ever at the lady's command as a companion, either at home or abroad.

Mrs. Dinsmore had few resources within herself, was a martyr to ennui, and could not bear to be alone. Mildred esteemed it both a duty and a pleasure to do all in her power to add to the comfort and enjoyment of her kind entertainers. She had succeeded thus far in doing so in some measure to all, from her uncle down to baby Enna.

The children had discovered weeks ago that Cousin Milly possessed an apparently inexhaustible fund of nursery tales and songs and could teach them many amusing games.

They would have been glad to monopolize her, and they entered many a complaint of the shortness and infrequency of her visits to the nursery.

Thinking of that now, she resolved to try to give them more of her time and attention. Perhaps she could mingle some instruction with the amusement she furnished them, and she would be very glad to do so, for her heart was filled with pity for the young things as she thought of the great difference between their mother and hers — the one absorbed in her own selfish pleasures, paying no attention to the cultivation of the minds and hearts of her children, the other giving herself with earnest, whole-souled devotion to seeking the best interests of her darlings, teaching and training them for happiness and usefulness here and hereafter.

"Precious mother, what a blessing to have been born your child!" Mildred mentally exclaimed as she thus dwelt upon the contrast between the two, recalling with tear-dimmed eyes the loving care that had surrounded her from her very birth and in which each brother and sister had an equal share.

While Mildred thus laid her plans, Mrs. Dinsmore was somewhat similarly employed. Reclining upon a softly cushioned couch in her boudoir, idly listening to the pattering rain against the window, she mused in discontented mood of Mildred and her unexpected resolve. It interfered with her schemes, for she had purposed filling the house with merry young company during the approaching Christmas holidays and making the two weeks one continual round of festivity.

To be sure, she could do so still, but Mildred's refusal to take part in much of the sport would throw a damper upon the enjoyment of the others, besides giving occasion for unpleasant criticisms.

Mrs. Dinsmore's vexations increased as she turned the matter over in her mind.

But a bright thought struck her, and starting up with something like energy, she exclaimed half aloud, "Why that's the very thing! And I'll do it at once."

"Hagar," she said, addressing her maid, "bring me my writing desk."

Chapter Ninth

*There's not a joy the world can give
like that it takes away.*

— Byron

"Dear me! Another dull, rainy, tedious day!" sighed Mrs. Dinsmore the next morning as she turned from the breakfast table, walked to the window, and looked out upon the gardens and fields where everything was dripping with wet. "Will the storm never end? There is no hope of visitors today, or of setting out to see anybody. I shall be literally eaten up with ennui."

"Here's Mildred," remarked Mr. Dinsmore. "I have always found her good company."

"Humph! She has no time to waste upon me."

"I am quite at your service, aunt," said our heroine pleasantly.

"Indeed! What's to become of your all-important studies?"

"They have already had two hours devoted to them this morning, besides two last night, so I think I have fairly earned the pleasure of your society for as much of the day as you care to have mine," returned the girl in a sprightly tone.

Mrs. Dinsmore looked surprised and pleased.

"You are an odd girl to rise early when you might just as well indulge in a morning nap," she said.

"I don't find it difficult if I have gotten to bed in good season the night before," said Mildred merrily. "I have been trained to it from childhood, my father being a firm believer in the old adage, 'Early to bed and early to rise, makes a man healthy, wealthy, and wise,' and it is really very pleasant after one is fairly up and dressed.

"Yes, and I dare say we would all be the better for it if we would follow your example," said Mr. Dinsmore.

"You are altogether mistaken as far as I am concerned," remarked his wife pettishly. "My best sleep is in the morning."

"I suppose people differ about that as well as in the amount of sleep they require," observed Mildred. "Some need eight hours, while others can do quite as well with only four."

"Yes," admitted her uncle, "constitutions differ, and I have no idea of asking my wife to give up her morning nap. There is a possibility of carrying the thing to an extreme. Remember that, Miss Milly," he added playfully, "and don't let that sensitive conscience of yours force you up at unchristian hours."

"And how am I to decide what are such, sir?" she asked, laughing.

Mildred devoted herself that day to her aunt's entertainment and with a success that restored her almost entirely to favor—at least for the time being.

The following day there was a slight abatement in the storm, and some gentlemen called.

One, a young man who had been her escort on several occasions and whom Mildred liked very much as a friend, inquired particularly for her.

He had come with an invitation open to a public ball to be given a week later by a military club of which he was a member and to ask that he might be her escort there.

Mildred declined with thanks.

He seemed much disappointed and pressed for her reasons.

"I have several, Mr. Landreth," she said, coloring slightly but meeting his eye unflinchingly. "I find that late hours injure my health; that is one. Another is that I have been brought up to consider it wrong to attend balls."

"Why more so than going to the theater?"

"I do not know that it is."

"Excuse me, but you go there."

"It is true. I have been several times, but that was wrong of me, and I do not intend to go again," Mildred said, humbly yet firmly, though the color deepened on her cheek and her voice trembled slightly.

The words had cost her no small effort, but she was glad when they were spoken. It seemed to lift a load from her heart and conscience.

Mr. Landreth looked full of regret and surprise.

"I am sorry," he said. "Would it be taking too great a liberty to ask why you think it wrong?"

It seemed a difficult and trying thing to undertake.

Mildred hesitated a moment, her eyes cast down, her cheeks burning. But, remembering the words of the Master, she answered, "'Whosoever, therefore, shall confess me before men, him will I confess also before my Father which is in heaven. But whosoever shall deny me before men, him will I also deny before my Father which is in heaven.'

"Because I profess to be a follower of the Lord Jesus Christ, and as such, to take His word as my rule of faith and practice. That word bids us 'whether, therefore, ye eat or drink, or whatsoever ye do, do all to the glory of God,' and I find it impossible to obey that command in attending such places of worldly amusement.'"

"You are very young to give up all pleasure," he said with an involuntary sigh. "One ought to have some happiness and some enjoyment in youth. I should say it would be quite time enough to resign all these things when we arrive at middle age."

"Ah, you quite mistake me, Mr. Landreth," she answered, looking up brightly. "I only resign a few miserable, unsatisfying pleasures for those that are infinitely higher and more enduring."

He gazed at her incredulously.

"Religion has always seemed to me a very gloomy thing," he said, "very good and valuable on a deathbed, no doubt, but—I should rather do without it till then, I must confess."

"I would not," she answered earnestly. "I want it to sweeten my life all the way through. Mr. Landreth, believe me, it does that as nothing else can. I have found it so in my own limited experience, and I know that my parents have in theirs, which has extended over so many more years.

"I have seen them wonderfully sustained by it under sore trials and have noticed that in times of happiness and prosperity, it more than doubled their joy and gladness. 'Godliness with contentment is great gain!'"

"Well, Miss Keith," he said after a moment's pause, "I think you deserve that it should be gain to you in some way, since you sacrifice so much for its sake."

"Ah, you are determined to consider it a sacrifice, I see," she returned, smiling. "And I deserve that you should," she added sorrowfully.

"Excuse me," he said, "I do not doubt your sincerity, but the Christians with whom I am most intimately acquainted seem to me anything but happy, if I may judge from their countenances and the gloomy austerity of their lives."

"Ah, if I could only show you my mother!" exclaimed Mildred. "If you could know her as I do, you would tell a different story!"

Mildred afterward repeated this last remark of Mr. Landreth's to her aunt.

"Yes," said Mrs. Dinsmore with an expressive shrug of the shoulders, "I know all about that, and you will understand it, too, when you have seen his aunt—or rather his uncle's wife—Mrs. James Landreth, and her house. By the way, we must call there. She called on me one day not long ago, when we were out."

"What is she like?" asked Mildred.

"Don't ask. Wait till you see her. No description could do her justice—at least none that I could give," Mrs. Dinsmore answered a little impatiently.

Mildred's curiosity was excited, and she was eager to make the proposed call.

After a few days' delay for good roads and good weather, she and her aunt set out, taking an early start, as they had a drive of some miles before them and intended to pay several other visits.

"The Landreths live in the suburbs of the city," Mrs. Dinsmore said, "and I have ordered Ajax to drive there first. I always like to get disagreeable things over."

"I wish," said Mildred, "that one might confine one's calls to those whom it is a real pleasure to visit."

"Of course, it would be very delightful if one could," said her aunt, "but there is no use talking about it. You can't tell people, 'I don't wish to keep up acquaintance with you because your society is not agreeable to me.'"

"No, of course not," returned Mildred, laughing. "Do you suppose Mrs. Landreth calls on us, too, because the customs of society require it?"

"Really, I can't tell. I know she doesn't enjoy it, because I am not her sort. I'm certain she looks upon me as a very worldly-minded, wicked woman — a kind of heathen, in fact. Perhaps she considers herself doing missionary work in coming to see me."

"The house and grounds are quite handsome," Mildred remarked with some surprise, as they alighted at Mr. Landreth's door.

"Outside," Mrs. Dinsmore returned significantly.

Mrs. Landreth was at home, and they were shown into the drawing room.

It was a spacious but rather dreary-looking apartment, very plainly furnished and almost wholly destitute of ornament, with the exception of a few old family portraits. The only really attractive objects in the room were a brightly blazing fire and a very fine painting over the mantel.

This last riveted Mildred's attention in a moment, and she exclaimed at its beauty.

"Yes," whispered Mrs. Dinsmore, "it's the one handsome thing in the house, and she is always at her husband to sell it."

"Why?" and Mildred's look expressed unfeigned astonishment at the very thought.

"Praise it to her, and you will hear all about it."

Their hostess entered. She was tall, angular, of sallow complexion, and strong-featured. Her black hair, streaked here and there with gray, was drawn straight back from a forehead crossed by many lines.

Caps were much worn even by youthful matrons of that day, but Mrs. Landreth had resorted to no such artifice to conceal from view the partially bald spot on the top of her head. Neither did the close-fitting, black gown hide one angle of her stiff, ungainly figure.

Her movements were very ungraceful, and her countenance was as solemn as might have befitted a funeral occasion.

"She is certainly far from pleasing in appearance," thought Mildred, furtively scanning the unattractive face and mentally contrasting it with the dear, bright, cheerful one that had made sunshine in her childhood home.

Mrs. Landreth's face served as a good foil even to Mrs. Dinsmore's faded beauty—a fact of which that lady was by no means unaware or intolerant.

The two conversed together for some minutes, Mildred sitting silently by. They were speaking of the weather and then of some acquaintance of whom she knew nothing. Not feeling interested, she unconsciously suffered her eyes to wander about the room.

"You do not find much to admire here?" Mrs. Landreth said interrogatively, turning abruptly to her. "There are no pretty trifles scattered here and there as at Roselands."

"I admire that beautiful painting over the mantel exceedingly," Mildred answered with a blush, turning her gaze upon it again. "Such a lovely, sunny landscape! It gives one a restful feeling just to look at it."

"Yes, it is a fine painting, but I have often told my husband that I think he committed a sin in putting so much money into an unnecessary luxury—something we could do perfectly well without. The Bible bids us be content with food and raiment, and we ought not to indulge ourselves in anything more or to spend much on them while there are so many deserving objects of charity in the world. That is why you find me so plain in my attire and in the furnishing of my house.

"Mr. Landreth holds different views and would like house and wife to look as well as those of his neighbors, as he often says, but I must act according to the dictates of my conscience."

"But don't you think it a duty to try to please your husband and make his home attractive?" Mildred asked modestly. "I know my mother considers it hers and her great pleasure also."

"Quite natural then that you should, but doubtless I am an older woman than she, and years should teach wisdom," rejoined Mrs. Landreth somewhat loftily.

"Yes, madam, I suppose they should, but do you think people are always wise just in proportion to their age?"

"Of course, not always. Mr. Landreth is older than I am.

"But now to return to the original topic. We are taught that we ought to practice self-denial and to give liberally to the poor. The interest of the money paid for that picture—five thousand dollars—would enable me to largely increase my benefactions, if I had it. And besides, how much useful work could the artist have done in the time he spent—wasted, one may as well say—in painting it."

"I cannot think the time was wasted or that God would have given him the talent if he were not to use it. I do not think it is wrong to surround ourselves with beautiful things if we have the means," ventured Mildred, still thinking of her mother's practice and the opinions she had heard her express.

Mrs. Landreth gave her a look that said as plainly as words, "I consider you a very opinionated and silly young person," and Mrs. Dinsmore arose to take leave.

"That woman," she remarked as she threw herself back in her carriage, "has done more to disgust me with religion than anybody or anything else! She is always parading her self-denial and benevolence and always looks as solemn as if it were a sin to laugh. She seems unhappy herself and anxious to make everybody else so. If that is Christianity, I want none of it! And I know that is just how Charlie Landreth feels!"

"But that isn't Christianity, Aunt," Mildred said earnestly. "And do you not know some Christians who are very different?"

"Yes, there's Mrs. Travilla at Ion, where we are going now. She is always cheerful, quite merry at times, and a great deal better woman, to my thinking, than Mrs. Landreth, though she doesn't appear to think so herself. In fact, she's too good for me, gives me an uncomfortable sense of my own inferiority in that respect."

"Are the Landreths poor?" asked Mildred.

"Poor! exclaimed Mrs. Dinsmore, laughing. "Wouldn't Charlie and his uncle be mortified if they could hear that question! Poor! No, indeed! Mr. Landreth could afford twenty paintings as costly as that, but he isn't allowed to enjoy one, and the house looks forlorn and comfortless from garret to cellar."

"And is she really benevolent?"

"She gives a great deal to missions, to the poor, and to the church, but I think it would be well for her to remember that charity begins at home and to bestow a little kindness upon her husband and his nephew. If they were beggars, she would perhaps think it worthwhile to pay some attention to their comfort. As it is, they get nothing from her but sermons and lectures on their worldliness and wickedness."

"But Mr. Charlie Landreth doesn't seem to me like a bad young man," said Mildred in surprise.

"He isn't," said Mrs. Dinsmore. "He's a thorough gentleman and has no vices. There isn't a finer young man, the country round. But he isn't pious. So, of course, she considers him a reprobate."

"I have heard my mother speak of Mrs. Travilla as a lovely Christian lady and an intimate friend of Aunt Eva," said Mildred, quite willing to introduce a new topic.

"Yes, and I always feel that she is still making comparisons, unfavorable to me, of course, between Mr. Dinsmore's first wife and myself. So, I can hardly be expected to be very fond of her."

"But isn't it possible that you may be mistaken, Aunt Isabel?"

"I'm not given to fancies," came the rather ungracious rejoinder.

There was a short silence broken presently by a query from Mildred.

"Has Mrs. Travilla any daughters?"

"No, only a son, and he's away in Europe. The families—ours and theirs—have always been intimate. Edward Travilla and Horace are inseparable companions, and they went to Europe together some time ago."

"It seems odd I should have been here so long without meeting Mrs. Travilla."

"She's been away. She went to the North with her son and did not return till quite recently. She called at Roselands the same day Mrs. Landreth did and inquired for you."

Mildred was greatly pleased with both Ion and its mistress.

The grounds were extensive, beautiful, and well cared for. The house was a fine old mansion, handsomely furnished, and abounded in tasteful ornamentation. There were beautiful articles scattered through its rooms—rare and costly bits of painting and sculpture. There were also less expensive adornments like singing birds and blooming plants and flowers, all showing a refined and cultivated taste and forming together a most harmonious and charming whole.

Mrs. Travilla was perhaps some years older than Mrs. Dinsmore, and with her, too, youthful bloom had fled. But it had given place to beauty of another and higher order—the illumination of a richly cultivated mind and heart.

She was attired with simple elegance and a due regard to her age, circumstances, and what best became her style of beauty. Her manner was simple and cordial, her conversation sprightly, and her voice low and sweet-toned.

"You resemble your mother," she said with a kindly smile, taking Mildred's hand in parting and gazing earnestly into her face. "I remember her well, for I saw a good deal of her on her visits to Roselands, and truly, to know her was to love her. Someday soon, if your aunt can spare you, you must spend a day with me, and we will have a long talk about her. I want to hear all you have to tell."

"Oh, I should be delighted!" Mildred exclaimed, her cheeks glowing and her eyes sparkling. Mrs. Travilla had found the way to her heart, and from that moment, they were fast friends.

CHAPTER TENTH

There is a friend that sticketh closer than a brother.

—PROVERBS 18:24

YOU FOUND MRS. Travilla a decided contrast to the other lady," remarked Mrs. Dinsmore as they drove down the avenue at Ion. "Pray, which do you think is right in her religious views?"

"There is no question in my mind as to which is more attractive," said Mildred, "or which seems to recommend her religion the most by her looks and ways. Mrs. Landreth's self-denial certainly appears commendable, but—oh, I confess that I am really puzzled and must take time to consider."

"Well, I hope you won't ever pattern your ways after Mrs. Landreth."

"No, never!" Mildred exclaimed with energy. "I know it cannot be right to make a home uninviting and cheerless. My mother has taught me better than that, both by precept and example."

"There is a letter for you, my dear," Mr. Dinsmore said, handing his wife and niece from the carriage.

"From whom?" she asked with interest.

"I have not opened it, but the address is in your sister Delia's hand."

"Ah! Then it is just the one I want."

At the tea table, Mrs. Dinsmore made a grand announcement to everyone.

"My two nieces, Juliet and Reba Marsden, are coming on a visit here. We may expect them tonight or tomorrow."

"Tonight?" said Mr. Dinsmore inquiringly. "They come by the stage, eh?"

"Yes. It passes at what hour?"

"Eight. Pomp," he said to the servant in waiting, "tell Aunt Phoebe to have a hot supper ready at quarter past eight."

"Young ladies, aunt?" asked Mildred, looking up with a bright, pleased face.

"Yes, they are eighteen and twenty. Company for you, I hope."

Mildred slipped away to her own room shortly before the time for the arrival of the stage. She had a lesson to prepare and a letter to write. She thought her aunt would most likely want to have her nieces to herself for the first hour or two of their visit. Besides, Mrs. Dinsmore had also expressed an intention to send them to bed promptly that they might be fresh for the ball that was to be held the next evening.

On the stairway, Mildred met her three younger cousins—Adelaide, Louise, and Lora.

"Study hour's just over, and we're going to the drawing room," they announced. "We've got permission to stay up and see our cousins when they come."

"That's very nice," she answered. "I hope to see them in the morning."

In the hall above, she passed Miss Worth on her way from the schoolroom to her own apartment. She was struck with the weary and sad expression on her face and paused for an instant, half inclined to offer her sympathy and ask if she could be of service in anything.

With a slight nod of recognition, the governess glided by, and the next moment Mildred heard her door close and the key turn in the lock.

"Poor thing! I dare say she is homesick!" thought Mildred, passing into her own room, which she found, as usual, very bright and cheery, with a good fire, a table with an astral lamp, books, and writing materials drawn up near it, and an easy chair on the farther side—the one inviting her to work, the other repose.

She had completely won Rachel's heart, and the young handmaiden took special pride and pleasure in arranging everything to "Miss Milly's" liking, and being always ready to wait upon her.

Mildred sat down at the table and opened her books.

"Two hours for these and my letter to mother, then to bed and to sleep that I may be able to rise early and secure the two morning hours for study before seeing those girls at breakfast," was the thought in her mind.

She set herself to her work with determined energy but in vain. She could not fix her attention. She studied the words again and again but without taking in their meaning. Miss Worth's sad face kept coming between her and the printed page.

"She must be very lonely. She needs a friend and a comforter," whispered the inward voice.

"But she might consider me an intruder, trying to pry into her private affairs and forcing a friendship upon her that she has never sought—and she is so much older than I," was the answering thought. "And she is only a governess. Aunt Belle evidently considers her quite beneath her friendship and might be displeased if I put her on an equal standing with myself."

But Mildred blushed to find herself influenced by such a motive. She, too, might be a governess someday, and she would be none the less a lady. It was an honorable and useful calling, and it ought to be considered far more creditable to earn one's bread thus than to be willing to live upon the labor of others.

"No," she exclaimed aloud, closing her book and pushing it from her. "That shall not hinder me! But ought I to go?"

Dropping her face into her hands, she sent up a silent petition. "Lord, show me! I desire to acknowledge Thee in all my ways, and I know Thou wilt fulfill Thy gracious promise to direct my paths."

Then she tried to put herself in Miss Worth's place. How utterly lonely the poor governess was among them all! Among, and yet not of, them. Mrs. Dinsmore would as soon have thought of sympathizing with an automaton as with any of the human creatures employed in her service. Her domestics were comfortably fed and clothed; Miss Worth's liberal salary was always punctually paid; and what more could any of them ask of her?

As Mildred mentally reviewed the events of the past weeks, she realized as never before how entirely apart from them all this one member of the family circle had been. Her presence was ignored in their familiar chat, except when it related in some way to her duties. Her wishes, taste, and convenience were never consulted; no interest was taken in her welfare; and no inquiries were made regarding her health or happiness, or as to whether her letters — usually handed to her at the breakfast table when the others received theirs — brought good news or ill.

Ah, now it came to Mildred's recollection that the morning's mail brought a letter for Miss Worth, and had she not looked a little paler than usual at dinner? And were there not traces of tears about her eyes?

Her hesitation was at an end. She was quite sure that if bad news had come to her, she would be glad to have the sympathy of even a child or a dumb animal. Only waiting to ask for wisdom to do and say the right thing, she rose and went out into the hall.

The stage had just driven up to the door, and the sounds coming from below told of the arrival of the expected guests — merry, girlish voices mingling with those of her aunt, uncle, and cousins.

She lingered a moment, thinking how pleasant it would be should those girls prove congenial companions to her. Then, going to Miss Worth's door, she tapped lightly on it.

A step came slowly across the room, and the door opened.

"Excuse me," Mildred said, blushing and hesitating. "I do not wish to intrude, but I thought you looked sad and had perhaps heard ill news or might be homesick and in need of a friend, even if it were one who had only sympathy to offer."

"Come in, won't you? It is very, very kind of you, Miss Keith. I did not expect it, and—and I do want a friend," she answered in hurried, tremulous tones. Miss Worth stepped back to allow her visitor to move into the room, then closed the door and set a chair for her near the fire.

A writing desk stood open on the table, an unfinished letter lying upon it.

"I'm afraid I have disturbed you," Mildred said, glancing at them. "You are busy?"

"No, I found I could not say what I wished, or perhaps did not know what I wanted to say," the governess answered with a dreary sigh.

Silence fell between them for some moments, Miss Worth, who had resumed her seat, gazing abstractly into the fire, while Mildred was trying to think what to say, silently asking to be directed. But she was not the first to speak.

"Does life ever seem to you a weary road to travel, Miss Keith, a burden that you would be glad to lay down forever?" asked the governess. "But I forget. You are so young and so happy that you can know nothing of such an experience. At your age, I was merry and light-hearted, too—as well I might be—at home in my father's house and abundantly supplied with comforts and luxuries without thought or care of mine. Ah, times are sadly changed with me and all who are nearest and dearest to me. But excuse me! I have no right to thrust my private griefs upon you."

"Please don't feel so," Mildred said, sympathetic tears springing to her eyes. "I cannot tell you how sorry I am for you! How I would like to comfort you! I know it is sometimes a relief and comfort just to pour out our sorrows to a fellow creature. And, oh, Miss Worth, I wish you knew what a comfort it is to tell them all to Jesus!" she added, low and feelingly.

"Is it? Do you think He can hear? That He listens? That He cares?"

The look that accompanied the questions was half eager, half skeptical, and full of unexpressed longing.

"I have not the least doubt of it," Mildred answered with earnest conviction in her tones. "'God over all blessed forever,' He is everywhere present. He has, as He himself declared, all power given unto Him in heaven and in earth; and He is so full of love and compassion that He deems nothing that concerns his children, one way or another, too small for His attention. He would not have even the little children turned away when the parents brought them to Him, and He cares for even the sparrows.

"'Are not two sparrows sold for a farthing? And one of them shall not fall to the ground without your Father. But the very hairs on your head are all numbered. Fear ye not, therefore, ye are of more value than many sparrows.'"

"But I am not one of His children," sighed the governess. "I have paid no attention to these things, Miss Mildred. I did not seek Him in my days of prosperity, and I cannot expect Him to care for me now in my adversity."

"But He is so loving and compassionate, so ready

to forgive. He proclaims Himself 'the Lord, the Lord God, merciful and gracious, long-suffering and abundant in goodness and truth, keeping mercy for thousands, forgiving iniquity, transgression, and sin.

"'Come now and let us reason together, saith the Lord. Though your sins be as scarlet, they shall be as white as snow; though they be red like crimson they shall be as wool.' Jesus said, 'Him that cometh to me I will in no wise cast out.' You say you want a friend, Miss Worth, and there is none other that can compare with Jesus in love and tenderness, in power and willingness to do all you need."

"A friend," repeated Miss Worth absently, more as if thinking aloud than talking to her visitor. "Yes, that is what I need and what I have been longing for for days and weeks, more especially tonight. But," she said, turning her face abruptly toward Mildred, while her voice took a touchingly pathetic tone, "I know not how or where to find the One you speak of, nor can I believe that He would receive me if I did. Why would He care to help and comfort me? Why should he?"

"I don't know, except that He is so good, so kind, and so loving!" Mildred said, her eyes shining. "But dare you doubt His word? The word of Him who tells us that He Himself is the truth?"

"Does He say that?"

"Yes, 'I am the way and the truth and the life.' Oh believe His love—the love of Christ, which passeth knowledge! 'Herein is love, not that we loved God, but that He loved us and sent His son to be the propitiation for our sins.'"

"Ah, but am I included in that word 'our'?"

"'Come unto me all ye that labor and are heavy laden and I will give you rest.' 'Whosoever will, let him take the water of life freely.' Could invitations be more comprehensive?"

"No, I think not. But how, Miss Mildred, how shall I come? I was not religiously brought up and am very ignorant on these subjects."

"'With the heart man believeth unto righteousness.' 'Believe unto righteousness.' 'Believe on the Lord Jesus Christ and thou shalt be saved.'"

"But what am I to do?"

"'Let the wicked forsake his way, and the unrighteous man his thoughts; and let him return unto the Lord, and He will have mercy upon him;'" quoted Mildred. "'And to our God, for He will abundantly pardon,' 'only believe'; 'for by grace are ye saved, through faith; and that not of yourselves; it is the gift of God. Not of works, lest any man should boast.'

"Do you not see that Christ has done it all? He has kept the law for us, borne its penalty in our stead, and now offers us the justification of our persons, the sanctification of our natures, and adoption into God's family all as a free gift—the purchase of His blood. We cannot merit it, we cannot buy it; it is 'without money and without price.' All we can do is accept the offered salvation and, forsaking every other hope and trust, lean wholly upon Jesus."

Miss Worth seemed lost in a sad, perplexing thought, while Mildred tried to make a clearer statement than before.

"It is so simple and beautiful, God's precious plan of salvation," Mildred said in conclusion. "We need only to give ourselves unreservedly to the Lord and trust wholly in Him. Jesus said, 'This is the work of God, that ye believe on Him who He hath sent.' And of His sheep, He says, 'I give unto them eternal life; and they shall never perish, neither shall any pluck them out of My hand.'"

"Yes, but I want a friend now—for this life with its cares, troubles, trials, and perplexities. Does He promise that?" asked the governess with a wistful, longing look.

"Oh, yes, yes, indeed! In very many places," Mildred said. "'This poor man cried and the Lord heard him and saved him out of all his troubles.'"

"'He shall deliver thee in six troubles; yea in seven there shall no evil touch thee.'

"'Call upon Me in the day of trouble: I will deliver thee, and thou shalt glorify Me.'

"'Cast thy burden upon the Lord and He shall sustain thee.'

"'Be careful for nothing; but in everything by prayer and supplication with thanksgiving, let your requests be made known unto God. And the peace of God which passeth all understanding, shall keep your hearts and minds through Christ Jesus.'"

Again a few moments of profound silence passed while Miss Worth seemed to be thinking deeply. Then, turning to Mildred, she said, "I cannot express my sense of kindness, and—" she paused, hesitated but went on hurriedly and with emotion, "I will seek this Friend of whom you have been speaking, for I sorely need one such a one. But you," she continued with increasing emotion, "you have so generously offered your sympathy yet refrained with true delicacy from showing the least curiosity in regard to my troubles. But it would be a relief to confide in you to some extent, if—if you would care to listen."

"I should be very much interested and very glad to be of service," Mildred answered gently. "And I think I need not assure you that your confidence will be sacred."

"No, I am quite certain of that," returned Miss Worth. She then went on to give a slight sketch of her past life—or rather of some parts of it, for she did not deem it necessary, or wise, to tell of all the trials which had fallen to her lot.

Her father, she said, had been in the early part of his career a very successful businessman, and in her childhood and youth, she was surrounded with luxury. But reverses came, loss followed loss, till they were reduced to absolute poverty. Then her father died, and the burden of her mother's support, as well as her own and that of a younger sister, fell upon her.

There was an older sister, who had been married for some years, but her husband was dissipated and worthless, and she had several little children to provide for as best as she could. The mother and Delia, the younger sister, lived with her, but Miss Worth paid their board and clothed them.

The letter received today had been from her married sister and drew a sad picture of toil, privation, and bitter disappointment. Her children were sick; her husband came home drunk every night to threaten and abuse her; her mother fretted continually over their reverses and her own ailments, fancied or real; and Delia was dissatisfied because she could not dress like other girls in the school she attended. The letter wound up with a request for a loan and a hint that the sum paid for board for her mother and sister was too small. Also, a little note was enclosed from Delia, asking, indeed almost demanding, money for the purchase of a new dress.

But of these Miss Worth said nothing.

Mildred was full of genuine sympathy and showed it in a way that was soothing and comforting.

Yet, after she was gone, the burden rolled back upon the heart of the poor, lonely governess. She sat long over the fire, head bowed upon her breast, vainly striving to solve the perplexing problem of how she was to meet all the demands upon her slender purse.

Her disposition was noble and self-sacrificing. She would have willingly denied herself all superfluities in dress so that her mother might not miss her accustomed luxuries, or Delia go without finery, or Mrs. Marks and her children be overworked or underfed. But it would not do. Mrs. Dinsmore's governess must be far from shabby in her attire.

CHAPTER ELEVENTH

Self is the medium least refined of all,
Through which Opinion's searching beam can fall;
And passing there, the clearest, steadiest ray,
Will tinge its light, and turn its line astray.

— MOORE

IT WAS AT the breakfast table the next morning that Mildred had her first sight of the newcomers. They were late in making their appearance, excusing themselves on the grounds of fatigue from their journey of the previous day.

Juliet, the elder of the two, was an extremely sentimental young lady — tall and thin with a fair complexion, pale auburn hair, and faded blue eyes.

The other, Reba, was a noisy, rattling, romping, pert young miss with staring black eyes, black hair straight and coarse, and a muddy complexion, which she strove with very limited success to conceal with powder and rouge. She prided herself on being a good shot with a pistol and not afraid to mount the wildest horse that could be found.

Her talk was of horses, dogs, race courses, and shooting matches, while her sister's was of beaux, parties, and dress.

Juliet had a great deal to say about her summer at Saratoga and the gentlemen she had met there, especially a certain titled foreigner, whom she spoke of as "that charming, fascinating Count de Lisle."

It came out in the course of the morning that she had heard from him since her return home in the fall and would not be surprised if he should follow her to Roselands.

"Pa won't like it if he does," remarked Reba. "He thinks he's a fortune hunter with nothing to recommend him but his title and that very likely it is all a pretense. I am inclined to think pa is right, and that the fellow is not even a foreigner."

"As if your opinion was of the least consequence!" sneered her sister. "I consider both you and pa extremely uncharitable to indulge in such suspicions. I have seen a good deal more of the Count than either of you, and he is a delightful man."

"Well, don't waste your time disputing, girls," interrupted Mrs. Dinsmore. "You have yet to decide what you will wear tonight."

They were now in the dressing room appropriated to the sisters during their stay. Mildred was with them, Mrs. Dinsmore having invited her in that they might have the benefit of her taste.

A quantity of finery was spread out upon the bed, table, and chairs, and presently the four were deep in consultation on the all-important subject.

Mildred was gifted with artistic taste in dress and great facility in giving form and shape to her conceptions by the use of scissors and needle. She was also very obliging, and having fallen today into the hands of those who were selfishly unscrupulous about imposing upon someone's good nature, she was given little rest until the two girls were fully attired for the ball.

They surveyed themselves with delight, and indeed both looked, for them, remarkably well. Juliet wore a white gauze over pale blue silk and a few white blossoms from the greenhouse in her hair. Reba was in black silk with a black lace overskirt looped with scarlet ribbons, and her hair was trimmed with flowers of the same brilliant hue.

She was in her wild spirits, dancing and pirouetting around the room and declaring that Mildred had laid her under lasting obligations. She'd had no idea how handsome she was, and it would be strange if she didn't make a conquest before the evening was over. Juliet heard it all with a contemptuous smile, while contemplating the reflection of her own charms in the glass with the self-satisfied thought that they far exceeded those of her sister.

"You are entirely welcome," said Mildred, "and I am very glad you are satisfied with the result of my labors. Now I must go to Aunt Belle, for I promised to put the finishing touches on her preparations."

"We'll go, too, and show ourselves to her," said Reba, and all three tripped merrily down the stairs into Mrs. Dinsmore's dressing room.

They found her resplendent in silk, lace, and diamonds. The costly gems hung from her ears and sparkled on her wrists, at her throat, and on every link of her watch chain. Mildred's task was to place a spray of them in her hair, already elaborately dressed by her waiting maid.

"Oh, you are splendid, Aunt Belle!" cried Reba, clapping her hands. "I declare, I believe you look younger and prettier than either of us."

"Don't turn flatterer, my dear child," said Mrs. Dinsmore, coloring with pleasure at the compliment and giving her mirror another glance of unmistakable satisfaction.

"Oh, you needn't pretend you don't know it," laughed Reba. "But now look at us and say if you're not proud of your nieces."

"Yes, indeed," Mrs. Dinsmore said after a moment's critical survey. "You are charming girls, both of you. Mildred, I think you deserve any amount of credit."

"Eh! What has she been about?" Mr. Dinsmore asked, coming in from an adjoining room. "Has she been superintending the dressing of these girls? Why, she is certainly a young lady of taste and quite a useful member of society."

"Decidedly prettier in her neat home dress than they in all their finery," he added mentally. Then aloud, he urged, "Come on, Milly, don't you begin to want to go along? It isn't too late to change your mind. We'll wait for you to dress."

"Thank you," she answered brightly, "but I have not changed my mind and really feel quite sure that I shall enjoy myself better at home."

"Such odd taste," laughed Reba.

"But perhaps she does not expect to pass the time alone," drawled Juliet with a significant look.

Mildred repelled the insinuation with dignity. "I expect no company but my books," she said, "and certainly desire no other."

She was entirely sincere, yet it did seem a little lonely as she sat by her fire in her own room after they had gone.

But she turned resolutely to her books, soon grew interested, and after a couple of hours spent in close study, retired to bed.

Only her uncle, Miss Worth, and the children met her at the breakfast table the next morning.

Mr. Dinsmore explained that his wife and her nieces were sleeping off their fatigue, adding, "The girls danced all night, and really it was near sunrise when they reached home."

"They must be very tired," Mildred said, "Aunt Belle and you, too, uncle."

"Yes, I think your plan was the wisest, after all. But what shall you do with yourself today? I fear you will be left quite to your own resources."

"I assure you I will be at no loss," she returned with a cheery smile.

The first thing in order after breakfast was a ride on which Adelaide, Louise, and Lora were her companions. The ride was a very enjoyable one, the morning being bright, clear, and not very cold.

On their return, as they cantered up the avenue, Adelaide exclaimed, "There's the Ion carriage at the door. What an early call Mrs. Travilla is making!"

But it was only a servant with a note for Mildred, an urgent invitation to her to drive over to Ion and spend the day.

"I send my carriage for you," wrote Mrs. Travilla, "hoping it may not return empty. Uncle Eben is a careful driver and will bring you safely, I think, and carry you back when you feel that your visit must come to an end. I should drive over myself, but I am confined to the house by a severe cold."

No more welcome invitation could have come to Mildred. Full of delight, she hastened to her room to change her riding habit for something more suitable for the occasion. That was the work of but a few moments, and leaving a message for Mrs. Dinsmore, who had not yet risen, she was presently rolling briskly along the road leading to Ion.

She anticipated a delightful day and was not disappointed. It was passed principally in Mrs. Travilla's boudoir and without other companionship and seemed to Mildred very much like a day at home with her mother, for this new friend was a woman of the same spirit and possessed very similar gifts and graces. She received her young guest with truly motherly warmth and tenderness of greeting.

The talk was first of Mildred's far-off home and the dear ones there, then of the better land and the dearest Friend of all that either possessed. While conversing of Him and His wondrous love, their hearts were drawn very close together.

"Mrs. Travilla," Mildred said, breaking a pause in the conversation, "there is someone I want you to help me pray for—someone who wants just such a kind, loving, powerful, everpresent Friend as Jesus."

"Yes, my child, I will," Mrs. Travilla responded with feeling. "We will unite our prayers, and He will know whom we mean, though I am ignorant of it, He whose precious promise is, 'If two of you shall agree on earth as touching anything that they shall ask, it shall be done of them of my Father which is in heaven.'"

"It *is* a precious promise," Mildred said, tears springing to her eyes. "And there are others. Oh, Mrs. Travilla, can you not guess whom it is that I want to plead it for? Some that I love, who are very kind to me but seem to care nothing at all about this Friend and to have no thought or concern for anything beyond this life."

"Yes, I know,' Mrs. Travilla said, pressing the girl's hand tenderly in hers. "And you may well believe that I have not known them all these years without often asking my dear Lord to reveal Himself to them in all His loveliness, and now I am very, very glad to have a helper in this."

They sat silent then for some minutes, then the adornments of the room, attracting Mildred's eye, reminded her of a question she had been longing to ask Mrs. Travilla.

Beginning with an account of her visit to Mrs. Landreth and the talk between them, in which Mrs. Travilla seemed interested, she went on to say with a smiling glance around the tasteful apartment, "I feel sure that you do not think as she does and that she is not right in her views or practices either, but I confess I am at a loss to know how to refute her arguments. So I have wanted to ask an explanation of your views. Do you think Mrs. Landreth is a really good Christian woman?"

"Yes, my dear, I do," Mrs. Travilla said. "She is beyond question very self-denying and benevolent, but I think she forgets that we are to 'adorn the doctrine of God our Savior in all things' and so fails to recommend it as she might to others, particularly her husband and his nephew.

"I quite agree with your mother that it is a wife's duty to study the comfort and happiness of her husband in everything that she can without violating the plain commands of God.

"Mrs. Landreth and I take different views on the question of the best way to help the poor. She gives money, and I let them earn it, paying them liberally for their work. This plan encourages industry and honest pride of independence, while the other teaches them to be willing to be idle pensioners on the bounty of their richer neighbors.

"Mine certainly seems the more self-indulgent way," she added with a smile, "for my house is thus filled with pretty things, while Mrs. Landreth's is left very bare of ornaments, and yet I think mine is the better plan."

"I am sure it is," Mildred responded with an energy and positiveness that brought a musical laugh from the lips of her friend.

"And," resumed Mrs. Travilla, "we differ quite as decidedly on the question of dress—she considering it a duty to spend as little as possible upon herself that she may have more to give, I thinking that those who have the means to do so without stinting their charities or driving hard bargains with their tradesmen should buy beautiful and expensive things in order to help and encourage manufacturers and render themselves, their families, and their houses attractive without being inordinantly extravagant.

"Surely God would not have implanted in us so strong a love of the beautiful and given so much to gratify it, if He meant us to ignore and repress it."

"No, surely not," Mildred said thoughtfully. "Oh, how good He is! How much He has given us to enjoy! There are so many beautiful sights and sounds in nature, so much to gratify the taste and smell—the perfume from your plants comes most pleasantly to my nostrils at this moment and the sweet song of that mockingbird to my ear. And I do so love the ocean's roar and the rippling of running water. Does it not seem like a slander upon the God of love to teach that He would have us spend all our time, effort, and means on those things that are utilitarian only?"

"It certainly does, and yet are not some of these things which some condemn as mere indulgences really useful after all? The surroundings affect the spirits, and they in turn the health and therefore the ability to work. Grand or beautiful scenery has often an inspiring or soothing effect, and their pictured representations offer the same to some extent."

"And just so with a sweet and noble face, and what a lovely one that is," Mildred said, turning her eyes toward a painting on the opposite wall.

"Yes," returned her friend, "I love to lie on my couch and gaze upon it when not able to sit up. It has been a comfort and help to me in many an hour of pain or sadness. Ah, who shall say that an artist's work is a waste of time—when his pencil is devoted to the reproduction of the good and the beautiful—or that his God-given talent is not to be improved?"

Then she drew Mildred's attention to various other paintings and pieces of fancy work, to each of which she had a story attached, generally of a struggle with poverty and want on the part of the one of whose talent and skill it was a specimen.

These tales were told in no boastful spirit, yet Mildred learned from them a valuable lesson on the best use of wealth and how much good might be done with it, in the way of lending a helping hand to those who needed assistance or to lift them out of an otherwise hopeless poverty. She learned well how this could be accomplished without sacrificing a praiseworthy pride of independence.

CHAPTER TWELFTH

O credulity,
Security's blind nurse, the dream of fools.

— MARON

MRS. DINSMORE CARRIED out her plans of filling her house with company during the holidays. They were mostly young people, and the time was spent in a constant round of festivities.

In these, Mildred bore some share, for she thought it right that she should do her part in entertaining her aunt's guests. Nor did her conscience at all forbid innocent recreation at proper times and seasons, though she could not consent to make mere amusement the business of her life.

Some half a dozen or more of the neighboring gentry were invited for the whole fortnight, while others came for an evening, a day, or two or three days. On Christmas Eve and New Year's night, large parties were given.

It was on the latter occasion that Mildred noticed for the first time among the guests a very handsome man who was apparently about thirty years of age but was an entire stranger to her.

His broadcloth and linen were of the finest, and a magnificent solitaire diamond adorned the little finger of his right hand. He wore an imperial and heavy moustache, and something foreign in his look and manner, as well as the fact that he seemed to be paying assiduous court to Juliet, suggested to Mildred that he was perhaps the Count de Lisle, of whom she had heard her make such frequent mention.

She was not long left in doubt as to that, for the next moment, Reba whispered his name in her ear, adding, "Juliet is in seventh heaven, of course."

"There is something sinister in the expression of his face," thought Mildred, turning away. "I do not like it. Yet, it is strangely familiar, too. Where can I possibly have seen it before?"

His attention had been attracted to her, and he inquired of Juliet, "Who is that pretty girl in pink and white!"

"Pretty!" returned Miss Marsden with a scornful toss of the head. "I cannot say that I admire her style. She's a Miss Keith, a sort of faraway niece of Uncle Dinsmore, a Northern girl and poor, I imagine, for her father's a country lawyer with a very large family."

Juliet was absolutely ignorant of Mr. Keith's circumstances, but it suited her plans to make it appear that she was no heiress and quite her own inferior in the matter of wealth, whatever she might be in looks.

"Do not be offended, my angel," he whispered, bending over her and speaking with a slightly foreign accent, which she had again and again extolled to Reba as perfectly delicious. "I meant not that she was half so beautiful or charmant as yourself."

"Ah, Count, you are a sad flatterer," she returned with a simper.

"No, no! Pardon the contradiction, Miss Juliet, but de truth is nefer flattery."

"A penny for your thoughts, Miss Keith," said a voice at Mildred's side.

"Good evening, Mr. Landreth," she replied, turning toward the speaker. "You are welcome to them gratis. I am wondering where I have seen Miss Marsden's admirer before tonight, or if it is only a resemblance, real or fancied, to someone else that I see in him."

"I cannot tell, indeed," he said, furtively watching the man for a moment, "but there is something I see in his face that would make me sorry to see him ingratiating himself with a lady friend of mine."

"Excuse me, but I must ask you to move, as we are going to dance and want the sofa behind you put out of the way," said Reba, coming up to them with two servants.

"Certainly," Mildred said, taking Mr. Landreth's offered arm.

They passed down the room and out into the conservatory beyond.

"Are you engaged for the first set?" he asked.

"No, nor for any other," she answered with a smile. "I do not dance, Mr. Landreth."

"It is not too late to begin, Miss Keith," he remarked persuasively.

"No, it is too soon."

"You don't think it wrong, here in your home, as it were?" he queried in surprise. "It is different, is it not, from attending a ball?"

"Yes, but I might grow so fond of it as to want to go to balls. I think it safest for me to simply avoid the temptation."

Sets were forming as they returned to the drawing room, and Miss Worth, who had been sent for to play the piano, was just entering by another door.

She had kept apart from the guests, spending almost all of her time in her own room, so that Mildred had seen very little of her for some days past.

Mildred noticed on the instant of her entrance that she was looking pale and worn, then that her pallor suddenly increased to ghastliness, as on stepping in she came face to face with Juliet and the Count in the nearest set, standing side by side.

He, too, started slightly and turned pale for a moment, as his eyes met those of the governess. But neither spoke, and pushing hastily past him, she sat down at the instrument.

She felt herself reeling in her seat and thought she should fall to the floor. Everything seemed to be turning around, but conquering her emotion by a great effort, she ran her fingers over the keys and dashed off into a lively dancing tune.

Her head was in awhirl, and a mist swam before her eyes so that she could not see the notes, but her fingers flew so fast that the dancers were soon panting for breath in their efforts to keep pace with the music.

"Not so fast, Miss Worth! Not so fast!" called several voices. But though for an instant she may have slackened her speed, the next she was rattling on as before.

Set after set had been danced, Juliet and the count taking part in them all, and now he led her panting to a seat.

"I like not zose tunes so well as some others," he remarked. "May I claim se privilege to speak to ze player zat she choose something else and not play quite so rapid?"

"Oh yes, certainly," smiled Juliet sweetly.

Miss Worth was turning over her music in search of a waltz someone had called for when a voice spoke at her side — a voice that made her start and shiver, though she did not look round.

"Your execution was von leetle bit too rapid for us," it said in an ordinary tone. Then in a whisper, the lips close to her ear, "Meet me half an hour after the company disperses behind the clump of evergreens at the foot of the avenue."

"Yes," she answered almost under her breath and without so much as turning her head.

She saw as in a nightmare a white hand, too large to be a woman's, with a solitaire diamond sparkling on the fourth finger, busied among the sheets of music before her. Then it vanished, her strained ear catching the faint echo of the retreating step.

She kept her eyes on her notes, her fingers wandering mechanically over the keys and calling forth low, soft strains of music while the dancers moved out into the refreshment room. She kept it up unceasingly until they returned and changed to a waltz in obedience to directions, as couples began taking their places on the floor. How long it lasted, she did not know. It seemed an age of suffering to her before she found herself again alone in the solitude of her own room.

As she entered, the clock on the mantel struck two. She glanced at it and sank into a chair by the fire.

"Half an hour," she sighed heavily, shivering and crouching over the blaze. "What an age to wait, and yet I'm afraid not long enough to let them all get to bed and asleep. What if I should be seen!"

She dropped her face into her hands with a low groan. It was some minutes before she lifted it again for another glance at the clock—a wan, weary, and haggard face, full of dread and distress, but with no tears in the burning eyes.

Slowly the moments dragged along till at last the minute hand pointed to the half hour, then she rose, wrapped herself in a large dark shawl, putting it over her head, listened at the door for a moment to make sure that all was quiet, then glided softly down the stairs. She let herself out a back door and, creeping along close to the wall of the house, then in the shadow of the trees that lined the avenue, gained at length the clump of evergreens at its farther end.

A biting north wind swept the hard, frozen ground and rustled the dry leaves at her feet as she stood leaning against a tree in an intensely listening attitude. It seemed to pierce to her very vitals, and shuddering and trembling with the cold and nervous dread, she drew the shawl more closely about her while straining her eyes through the gloom to catch a glimpse of him whom she had come to meet, for there was no light save that shining in the winter sky.

She had waited but a moment when a stealthy step drew near and a tall form wrapped in a cloak stood before her.

"Here first?" he said in a cautious whisper.

"Yes," she answered in the same low key and with a sudden catching of her breath. "Oh, why are you here? Why?"

"For my own advantage," he answered half defiantly. Then, in a threatening tone, he added, "And you'd better have a care how you betray me."

"I have no desire to do so," she returned with a weary sigh. "But you must go, and at once. You will ruin me if you stay. You must see that."

"Pooh. I see no such thing. And must is a word you have no right to use to me. Keep your mouth shut, and all will go well."

"What is your object in coming here?"

"Plain enough, I should think," he answered with a sneer.

"You are deceiving that silly girl and intend to marry her, simply for her money?"

"Exactly. Who needs money more than I?"

"And how long will it take you to squander it?"

"Depends upon how much there is," he returned with a sardonic laugh.

"And your luck at the gaming table," she said bitterly. "You are acting most dishonorably toward the girl. She wouldn't look at you if she knew—"

"That I am an American-born citizen, eh? Well, am I any worse for that?"

"Not for that—not in my esteem. But you know, you *know* that is not all, nor the worst by a great deal!" she cried in a tone of suppressed agony. "And you ask me to stand by and see you deceive this girl to her ruin, never stretching out a finger for her help! I cannot do it. I will not! Go! Go! You must! You must never show your face here again!"

"Be quiet!" he said angrily, for in her excitement, she had raised her voice to a dangerously high pitch. "And look at home," he went on. "Remember that you are partly responsible for my ruin, and that you, too, are sailing under false colors."

"But not to the injury of anyone and not with any evil intent," she answered, clasping her hands beseechingly. "And if you drive me from here, Harry, you will be taking the bread out of our mother's mouth. It is surely enough that you do nothing for her support yourself."

"I'll help with that when I have secured this girl and her money," he said with an evil laugh. "Just you keep quiet and all will go well. Keep my secret, and I'll keep yours."

She leaned back wearily against the tree, clasping her hands more tightly over her throbbing heart. Tears sprang to her eyes and her lips trembled, but no sound came from them.

"Well?" he cried impatiently.

"Harry," she said, very low and tremulously, "I have been reading a good deal lately in an old book — one whose teachings we used to respect in our innocent childhood — and it tells me that 'the way of transgressors is hard'; that though 'hand join in hand, the wicked shall not be unpunished'; that there is such a thing as sinning away your day of grace. And it says,

'Seek ye the Lord while He may be found; call ye upon Him while He is near.' Oh, Harry, turn from your wicked ways before it is forever too late. There is mercy even for you, if you will turn now."

Spellbound with astonishment, he had heard her thus far in absolute silence, but now he interrupted her with a savage oath.

"I didn't know you'd turned pious," he sneered. "And I didn't come here to be preached to. If you know what's for your good, you'll keep quiet. That's all I have to say, and now I'm off. I can't stand here catching my death of cold."

He was turning away, but she grasped a fold of his cloak.

"Harry," she said in a choking voice, "we used to be fond of each other: I was very proud of my handsome brother, and—and we've been parted for five years!"

"That's true, Gerty," he said in a softened tone, turning back and throwing an arm about her waist. Let's kiss and be friends."

"Harry," she whispered, clinging to him, "do you know anything of—of *him*?"

"No, and don't want to!" he answered savagely. "You're not fool enough to care for him now?"

"Women are fools," was all she said in reply.

They parted, he disappearing in the direction of the road, and she creeping back to the house and regaining the shelter of her own room, fortunately without meeting anyone on the way.

She was tired—oh, *so* tired, her strength scarcely sufficient to bring her to the desired haven. But even

131

there she could not rest. She did not undress or lie down but crouched beside the fire, her hands clasped about her knees and her head bowed upon her breast, while the monotonous ticking of the clock told off the weary seconds and the smoldering embers burned out, leaving nothing but the cold ashes on the hearth.

CHAPTER THIRTEENTH

In desert wilds, in midnight gloom,
In grateful joy, in trying pain,
In laughing youth, or nigh the tomb,
Ah! when in prayer unheard or vain?

— Eliza Cook

THE COLD, GRAY dawn of the winter morning was stealing in at the windows as at last, sighing heavily, the governess lifted her head with a returning consciousness of her surroundings.

How dreary it all looked in the dim, uncertain light—the disordered room, the fireless hearth—fit emblem, as it seemed, of the cold, almost dead heart within her.

Life was like a desert at that moment—a rough, weary road where thorns and briars constantly pierced her tired feet. Why should she stay? Why not lie down and rest in a quiet grave?

She rose slowly, stiff from the constrained posture she had held for so long, and dragged herself across the room. Opening her wardrobe door, she took from the shelf a vial labeled "laudanum." She held it a moment in her hand.

"It is only to go to sleep," she said half aloud, "to go to sleep and never wake again. Never? Ah! if I could be sure, *sure* of that!"

"'And the smoke of their torment ascendeth up forever and ever.' 'Where their worm dieth not, and the fire is not quenched.'"

With a shudder, she put it hastily back, locked the door, and threw herself upon the bed.

"Oh, God, forgive me!" she cried. "Keep me, keep me, or I shall do it yet! And then—forever and ever! No space for repentance, no coming back!"

At length, tired nature found temporary relief in the heavy, dreamless slumber of utter exhaustion.

Hours passed and still she slept on, hearing not, nor heeding the sounds of returning life in the household.

They were very late after their long night of revelry. Breakfast was not on the table till ten o'clock, and even then no one answered the summons but the master of the house and Mildred.

The children had taken their morning meal two hours before.

"An unexpected pleasure, this is, Milly, my dear," was Mr. Dinsmore's greeting.

"What, uncle, you did not surely expect me to be still in bed!"

"Well, no, but I thought you would be looking fatigued and worn, but instead, your face is as fresh and fair as a rose just washed with dew and as bright as the morning."

"And why should I not, if sufficient rest alone will do it?" she said laughingly. "I retired promptly at twelve and had my eight hours of sound, refreshing sleep."

"Ah, you are a wise little woman! Too sensible to let late hours rob you of health and good looks and make you old before your time. What is it Solomon says? 'Early to bed and early to rise?'"

"Oh, uncle, what a joke! There's no use in your pretending that you don't know any better than that," she answered merrily.

"Well, perhaps I do, but he certainly does say something about lying late in bed."

"Several things. One occurs to me now. 'Love not sleep, lest thou cometh to poverty. Open thine eyes, and thou shalt be satisfied with bread.' But it cannot mean that we should not take needful rest?"

"Oh, no, of course not! There's nothing gained by that. But where's Miss Worth?"

"She has not joined us since the house has been so full of guests. I think she has been taking her meals with the children in the nursery."

"Ah, yes. I presume so, but I had forgotten it, and it struck me that she might be ill. I thought she was looking badly last night. Did you notice it?"

"Yes, I did. I will inquire about her," Mildred said, remembering with a pang of self-reproach how ghastly a face the governess had worn on taking her seat at the piano.

She might be very ill, unable to call for help, neglected by the sleepy maids, and Mildred herself had been up for two hours and should have gone to her door to inquire.

She went immediately on leaving the table, her alarm and anxiety increasing on the way there by the information, gleaned from one of the servants, that Miss Worth had not been present at the nursery breakfast.

Mildred rapped lightly, then louder. Receiving no answer, she tried the door. It opened, and she stole softly in.

Miss Worth lay on the outside of the bed, still dressed as she had last seen her—in the drawing room at the piano—and sleeping heavily. Her face was very pale and distressed, and she moaned now and then as if in pain.

She had nothing over her, but a heavy, dark shawl lay on the floor beside the chimney. Mildred picked it up and spread it over her, drew down the blinds to shut out the glare of the sun, rang for the maid, and while waiting for her, moved quietly about the room putting things in their places.

"It is very cold in here, for the fire is quite out and must be made up at once," she whispered, meeting the girl at the door and motioning her to make no noise. "Go bring up wood and kindling."

"De governess sick, Miss Milly?" queried the servant, sending a curious glance in the direction of the bed.

"I don't know, Dinah, perhaps only tired, for she was up very late last night. But she is asleep and must not be disturbed," said Mildred as she motioned her imperatively away.

It was not till an hour later that Miss Worth finally stirred from her slumber and woke to find a cheerful fire blazing on the hearth and Mildred beside it quietly knitting.

She put down her work hastily, rose, and came forward as she perceived the governess' eyes fixed upon her in a sort of perplexed surprise.

"Excuse the intrusion," Mildred said, "but I thought you seemed ill and was afraid you might need help. I hope your sleep has refreshed you and that you will let me order the breakfast they are keeping hot for you in the kitchen."

"Thank you, I cannot understand such kindness to me," Miss Worth said huskily. "I was simply very tired—not sick, I think—and I suppose the sleep has done me some good."

"And you will eat something?"

"I will try, since you are so good."

The effort was but indifferently successful, yet Miss Worth steadily refused to acknowledge herself on the sick list and insisted that she was able to work and must do so. Mildred went away, feeling troubled and anxious.

Left alone, Miss Worth took out her writing materials. Resting her elbows on the table, her face in her hands, she sat thus for a long time without moving, a heavy sigh now and then escaping her.

At last, she took up her pen and wrote rapidly for several minutes. Then, snatching up the paper, she tore it into fragments and threw them into the fire.

Another sheet shared the same fate, and seeming to give it up in despair, she rose and walked the floor.

"Oh, if I only knew what to do, what to say!" she moaned. "If he would but hear reason, if he would forsake his evil courses! And yet—oh, if I had a friend! Just one wise, true friend to advise and help me! But I dare not breathe my terrible fears to any mortal, and who is there that would care to listen?"

Her eye fell on the Bible lying there on the table, and with the sight came recollection of the texts Mildred had quoted to her.

She almost heard a gentle voice saying, "Come unto Me, and I will give you rest."

Falling on her knees, she cried to Him, "Lord Jesus, I do come! I give myself to Thee. Oh, I beseech Thee in Thy great mercy and loving kindness to help me in this, my hour of perplexity and distress!"

It is strange what a blessed calm can succeed the storm. She rose from her knees wondrously soothed and quieted. She had found a Friend who had pledged His word to help her and who had all power in heaven and in earth. What need she fear? "If God be for us, who can be against us?"

There might be trouble in store for her — great and sore trouble — but He would help her through it.

There was a sound of merry young voices in the halls without and on the stairway. A carriage had driven to the door, an open barouche, and presently she saw it going down the avenue and that Mr. and Mrs. Dinsmore and the three young ladies were in it.

The older children were away from home, as she knew, spending a few days at a neighboring plantation. The younger ones were probably in the nursery.

She watched the carriage till it was lost to sight far down the road. Then, turning from the window with the thought in her mind that it would be a blessing to Juliet Marsden, as well as herself, if it were taking her home to her father's care, she caught sight of a horseman coming from the opposite direction.

She stood still, scanning him narrowly as he turned in at the gate and came cantering up the avenue. As he drew near, she recognized him with a start of surprise, terror mingling with it at first but changing instantly to joy that he had assuredly missed the object of his visit.

It was her scoundrel brother. But in spite of all the distress and anguish of mind he was causing her, she was conscious of a thrill of sisterly pride in his handsome face and form and the grace and ease of his horsemanship.

She must seize this unhoped-for opportunity. There were motives she could urge which escaped her thoughts the previous night and that might, perhaps, have weight with him. Much now depended upon prompt action on her part.

She flew down the stairs and admitted him herself before he even had time to ring. Fortunately, no servant had perceived his approach.

He looked at her in extreme surprise.

"How is this?" he inquired with an ill-natured sneer. "Have you been promoted to the office of porter, then?"

"Hush!" she answered in an imperative whisper. "Come here," and she led the way into a little parlor close at hand.

"Excuse the impertinence, Madame, but I did not come to see you," he said angrily, as he followed her.

"I am well aware of that fact," she said in a calm tone of quiet firmness as she turned and faced him.

"Nevertheless, I believe I am the one, and the only one, you will see. And it is well, for I have something of importance to say."

"Where is Miss Marsden?" he demanded.

"Gone for a drive, and all the other ladies with her. Mr. Dinsmore also. The last of the guests left an hour ago, and we may chat for a good while without much fear of interruption."

"Suppose I don't choose to do so," he returned, straightening himself with a defiant air.

"Harry, you must hear me!" she said, laying a detaining hand upon his arm, for he was moving toward the door.

"That's a strong word, and one you've no right to use to me," he answered moodily, yet yielding to her determined will.

She pointed to a chair, and he sat down.

"Speak and be done with it," he said.

Tears sprang to her eyes, but she held them back.

"Are you mad, Harry, that you venture to return to this country?" she asked in an undertone, her voice trembling with excitement. "Can you have forgotten the danger that hangs over you?"

"It's trifling, considering all of the changes five years have made," he said with affected nonchalance. But his cheek paled.

"Don't deceive yourself. Don't trust to that. I recognized you at the first glance," she said with the earnestness of one determined to convince.

"Well, one of my own family would, of course, be more apt to do so than anyone else. And I was never known in this part of the country."

"No, but people travel about a great deal now. Northerners come to the South frequently, especially in the winter. You may, any day, come face to face with some old acquaintance who will recognize you and have you arrested. And then —" she hid her face and shuddered. "Oh, Harry," she cried, "I shall live in terror till I know you are safe on the other side of the ocean."

"I'll go in all haste when I have secured my prize," he said coldly.

"Give it up," she entreated. "You have no right to drag an innocent girl down to infamy with you. Better go and make an honest living by the labor of your hands."

"I wasn't brought up to that and infinitely prefer to live by my wits," he answered with an evil smile. "And they'll have to help me to the means to pay my passage to those foreign shores you so very highly recommend."

"Sell this," she said, pointing to the glittering gem on his finger. "It would surely bring more than enough for that."

"Paste, my dear, nothing but paste," he laughed. "Clever imitation, isn't it?"

"Ah, Harry, a fair type of its owner, I fear," she said sorrowfully.

"Thank you for the compliment," he answered with a bitter laugh. "Well, after all, it is a compliment, taken in the sense that I'm as clever an imitation of what Miss Marsden takes me for as this is of a real diamond. Perhaps she's as good a judge of the first article as you are of the other. Ha! Ha!"

"Harry," cried his sister, "are you utterly heartless? Have you no pity at all for the poor silly girl?"

"Pooh! Gertrude, I have to look out for myself, and other people must do the same. I tell you, it is a case of necessity," he answered doggedly.

"No," she said, "there cannot be a necessity for wrongdoing, and if persisted in, it must end at last in terrible retribution—both in this world and the next," she added in low, tremulous tones.

"I'll risk it," he said with an oath. "And as to the girl, why, she'd break her silly heart if I should forsake her," he added with an unpleasant laugh. "You've no idea how deeply in love she is."

"You are mistaken. She has no heart to break and loves nobody half so well as herself. She will never be the woman to stand by and comfort you in adversity; therefore, you will be doing a foolish thing to make her your wife, even though you consult your own interest alone."

At that, he only laughed, saying that as the girl's money was all he wanted, he didn't care whether she stood by him or not after he once got it into his possession.

She renewed her warnings and entreaties, urging every motive she could think of to induce him to give up his wicked designs upon Juliet Marsden and forsake all his evil courses. But it was in vain. His heart was fully set in him to do evil, and neither love of his mother and sisters, nor pity for the deluded girl, could move him.

Nor did fear of punishment deter him. He was no coward, he said, glorying in his shame and showing himself utterly devoid of wisdom. 'For the fear of the Lord, that is wisdom; and to depart from evil, is understanding.' And the Bible calls fools all those who make a mock at sin, despise instruction, and hate to depart from evil.

At length there was a sound of approaching wheels, upon which he exclaimed in a relieved tone, "There, you'd better go. It won't help you or me for us to be caught together."

"No," she assented, rising hastily. "I must go. Oh, Harry, think of what I've been saying and don't rush headlong to destruction!"

"There! I've had enough of it!" he retorted angrily. "I'll do as I please. And you, keep yourself quiet."

Chapter Fourteenth

Hoe poor a thing is pride!
The beauty you o'erprise so, time or sickness
Can change to loath'd deformity; your wealth
The prey of thieves.

— MASSINGER

THE MOST OPENHANDED hospitality having ever been the rule at Roselands, it was no difficult matter for Count de Lisle to get himself invited to stay to tea and spend the evening. In fact, it was long past midnight when he at last took leave of Juliet and went away.

The thud of his horse's hoofs as he galloped down the avenue brought a pale, haggard face to an upper window, but the dim light of the stars revealed nothing save the merest outline of the steed and his rider, and that but for an instant.

The watcher turned away, sighing to herself, "I cannot see him, but it must be he." She hastily crossed the room and stole noiselessly into the hall beyond.

The hours spent by him in dalliance with Juliet— they had had the drawing room to themselves since ten o'clock—had been to her, his much tried sister, a time of bitter anguish and fierce mental conflict.

How could she permit this wickedness? Yet how could she prevent it when the only way to do so was by exposing him — her brother?

It seemed a terribly hard thing to do, for she loved him and his disgrace was hers and that of the whole family.

She was sorely tempted to leave Juliet to the fate she seemed to be drawing upon herself by her egregious folly — that of becoming the wife of a spendthrift and one whose vices had led him to commit a crime against the laws of the land, the penalty for which was a term of years in the penitentiary.

It would be a sad fate but perhaps not undeserved by a girl who would rush into it in opposition to the known wishes and commands of her parents.

Harry had unguardedly admitted to his sister that he had no hope of winning the consent of either Mr. or Mrs. Marsden, that they were, in fact, so violently opposed to his suit that he dared not visit their daughter in her own home. But he had exultingly added that he was perfectly certain of his ability to persuade Juliet to elope with him and meant to do so sooner or later.

Well, should he accomplish that and escape to Europe with his prize, his family probably would not suffer any ill consequences. No one here knew his real name or had the slightest suspicion that Miss Worth was in any way connected with him, but she felt morally certain that in case Mrs. Dinsmore discovered the truth, her situation at Roselands was lost. She would be sent away without a recommendation, and it might be months before she could get employment elsewhere. And that meant beggary to herself and those nearest and dearest to her.

Surely no motive of self-interest urged her to stretch out a hand to save Juliet Marsden from falling into the snare spread for her unwary feet. Yet pity for the girl, a strong sense of justice, and more than all, a desire to do the will of her new found Friend prevailed over all selfish considerations. Thus, she fully determined to give the warning, though in a way to risk as little as possible, and for the last half hour, she had watched and waited for the opportunity.

Juliet came up the stairs with a light, quick step, and as she passed underneath the lamp swung from the ceiling, its rays, falling full upon her, gave to Miss Worth a moment's distinct view of her face.

It wore an expression of exultant joy: The cheeks were flushed, the eyes glittering, the lips smiling.

"He has offered himself and been accepted," was Miss Worth's conclusion. "There is no time to be lost." Stepping forward, she stood directly in Juliet's path, confronting her with a calm face and a determined air.

"What is the meaning of this intrusion?" asked Juliet, recoiling and regarding the governess with mingled anger and hauteur. "Will you be good enough to step aside and allow me to pass on to my own apartments?"

"Excuse me, Miss Marsden, but I must have a word with you," returned the person addressed, in low, distinct tones, not moving a hair's breadth from the position she had taken.

"Indeed!" was the scornful rejoinder. "Pray, who may you be to take such airs upon yourself? My aunt's governess, if I am not mistaken, a person with whom I can have nothing in common. Keep your communications for those in your own station in life. *Will* you step out of the way?"

"Not yet. Not till I have discharged my duty to you, Miss Marsden. I must speak a word of warning, for I cannot see you rushing headlong to destruction without crying out to you to beware, and I have no motive for doing so but pity for you."

Juliet's astonishment was unbounded. What could the creature mean? What indeed but to insult her.

"Pity for me!" she cried with withering scorn. "You, a poor dependent governess, pity me! Me, the daughter of a wealthy Kentucky planter and an heiress in my own right. Keep your compassion for such as want it. I want none of it!" She would have pushed past Miss Worth, but the latter laid a hand on her arm, not roughly but with determination.

"It is of Count de Lisle I would speak to you," she said almost under her breath. "No, I take that back, for he has no right to either the name or the title."

"How dare you!" cried Juliet with flashing eyes, shaking off the detaining hand and drawing herself up to her full height. "What do you know of him?"

"Far more than you do," returned the other calmly. "I have known him all his life, and I tell you he is not what you suppose—not what he gives himself out to be. He is a man without fortune or title—an American by birth and education. He is seeking you merely for your wealth."

"I don't believe a word of it! It's all a pack of lies that you have invented because you are envious of me. Stand out of my way and don't presume to speak to me again on this subject, nor any other."

So saying, the angry girl swept proudly past the humble governess, whom she regarded as a menial and an impertinent meddler in her affairs. Gaining her apartments, she shut and locked herself in with a noise that roused her sleeping sister.

"The impudent creature!" she muttered.

"Who?" queried Reba, starting up in bed. "Have you actually discovered that pa is right and your count a mercenary adventurer?"

"Nonsense! No, I've learned no such thing!"

"What then? Who is the impudent creature you are anathematizing?"

"Aunt Belle's governess. She actually waylaid me in the hall and forced me to stand still and listen while she uttered a warning against him, pretending that he was an old acquaintance of hers. I shall complain to aunt and have her turned adrift for her impertinence."

"Better not," laughed Reba. "'Twould only arouse suspicion against him. It must be very late. I advise you to wake up your maid and get ready for bed."

The encounter had left Miss Worth in quite as unamiable a frame of mind as that of her antagonist, for the insulting arrogance of Juliet's manner had sorely wounded her pride. It was hard to take such treatment from one who was her superior in nothing but the accident of wealth, and in fact decidedly her inferior in the higher gifts of intellect and education.

"I wash my hands of the whole affair. I will leave her to her fate," Miss Worth said to herself as she turned in again at her own door and secured it after her.

With that, she endeavored to dismiss the whole matter from her mind. She was exceedingly weary and must have some rest, and presently everything was forgotten in a heavy, dreamless sleep.

But with the first moment of wakefulness, the burden again pressed heavily upon her. She could not be indifferent to her brother's wrongdoing nor to the danger of his discovery, arrest, and punishment for his former crime.

But the holidays were over, and she must return to her duties in the schoolroom. Perhaps it was well for her that it was so, since it compelled her to give her thoughts to other subjects.

Still taking her meals in the nursery, she saw nothing of the lady guests till Mildred came in that afternoon with a recitation.

Mildred was quietly and steadily pursuing the course of study which she had laid out for herself, mingling to some extent in the employments and pastimes of those about her but contriving to retire early almost every night. By early rising, she secured the morning hours for the improvement of her mind—a season safe from interruption by her aunt and her nieces, as it was always spent by them in bed.

In fact, there was such an utter absence of congeniality between Mildred and the other two girls that they were generally better content to remain apart. And as Mrs. Dinsmore preferred the companionship of her own nieces, because of both the ties of kindred and harmony of taste and feeling, Mildred was left to follow her own inclinations with little hindrance from any of them.

But though continuing her studies, Mildred, because she felt that the governess was entitled to the full benefit of the holiday rest, had not during the past two weeks gone to her for assistance or with recitations.

She was glad that she might now do so with propriety, for since the episode of the previous morning, she had not been able to forget Miss Worth's pale, distressed countenance and was really very anxious about her.

She felt quite sure there was some deeper trouble than mere physical pain, and she had a longing desire to give sympathy and relief—a desire untainted by a touch of prying curiosity. That strengthened so greatly during the afternoon's interview that she was willing to give expression to it, doing so with extreme delicacy and tact.

When the business part of their interview was over, Mildred closed her books and rose to leave the room.

For a moment, Miss Worth was silent, her features working with emotion.

"You are very, very kind to me, Miss Keith," she said at last. "I wish I might confide fully in you, but you are so young, too young and free from care to understand my—" She broke off quite abruptly and with a groan, dropping her face upon her folded arms on the table at which they had been sitting.

"Perhaps that is so," Mildred said in gently compassionate tones. "I could almost wish for your sake that I were older."

Miss Worth lifted her head, and with almost startling suddenness and a feverish eagerness in her tones, she asked, "Miss Mildred, where is Miss Juliet Marsden today?"

"She has passed the greater part of it in bed, I believe," Mildred answered in utter surprise.

"Has — has her lover been here since — since he left her last night?"

"The Count? No."

"Can you tell me if she is to go out tonight? And where? And who is to be her escort? Ah, I see you are wondering at my curiosity, and it is only natural that you should. But believe me, it is not the idle inquisitiveness it must seem to you," she went on rapidly and in anguished accents. "I do have a reason. There is much at stake. I — I have tried to be indifferent, to say to myself that it is nothing to me if — if that vain, silly girl should meet with the fate her folly deserves, but I cannot. I must try to save her — and him. Oh, if I could but save *him*."

And again she hid her face, while sobs shook her from head to foot.

"Him!" Mildred cried in increased amazement. "What is he to you? No, no, I do not ask that. I have no wish to pry into your secrets."

Miss Worth lifted her head and wiped away her tears.

"Thank you, for withdrawing that question," she said in a broken voice. "I cannot answer it, but — but this much I will tell you in the strictest confidence: I have known him in other days, and he is not what he professes to be. It would be absolute *ruin* to her!"

"Is that so?" Mildred said with a startled look. "Then surely you will warn her?"

"I have done so, Miss Keith, though it was like drawing my eyeteeth to do it. But my sacrifice was unappreciated, and my motives were misconstrued. I was treated with scorn and contempt, and have said to myself, 'I have a just right to be angry and indignant and shall leave her to her fate.'"

"But you will tell my uncle? He might be able to prevent the mischief by setting a watch upon them and forbidding the man to enter the house."

"No, no, I cannot betray him!" cried Miss Worth in a startled, terrified tone. "And you—you will respect my confidence, Miss Keith?"

"Certainly, but—surely you will not suffer Juliet to be sacrificed?"

"I have warned her," returned the governess coldly, "and since she refuses to heed, on her own head be the consequences."

It was Mildred's turn to be troubled and perplexed. She stood for a moment in anxious thought.

"Will you not make one more effort?" she said at length. "Would you not save him from this wrongdoing? May not the consequences be dreadful to him, too? May not her father take a terrible revenge, as men sometimes do on deceivers and betrayers of their daughters?"

Miss Worth started, and her wan cheek turned a shade paler.

"I had not thought of that!" she said, drawing a long breath. "Oh, what shall I do?"

They consulted together but with no more definite result than a mutual agreement to keep a strict watch upon the movements of Juliet and her pseudo-nobleman.

Mildred was again about to withdraw when Miss Worth stopped her.

"Pardon me, Miss Keith," she said. "But you have not answered my questions."

"They all go to the theater tonight, an, I happen to know Mr. Landreth is to escort Miss Juliet."

"Not the count? But she will meet him there. I am sure of it. You will not go, Miss Mildred?"

"To the theater? Oh, no!"

"Then I must go myself and watch them."

"Surely that is not necessary," reasoned Mildred. "Uncle, Aunt, Reba—all close at hand."

"Ah! perhaps not," assented the governess. "Possibly it is wiser to leave the task to them."

Mildred went to her room to ponder and pray over the matter, for she was sorely perplexed and more than a little anxious for Juliet.

She asked help and direction for herself and Miss Worth, and that the latter might be led to do her duty, however difficult and painful.

She wondered greatly what was the tie between her and this spurious count until it flashed upon her that his familiar look was a strong likeness to the governess. Then she knew it was that of relationship.

Her own duty in the affair formed a serious question in her mind.

She sorely wished Miss Worth's communication had not been made in confidence and that she were free to carry it to her uncle, who would, in that case, be sure to interfere effectually to save Juliet from falling prey to the schemes of this false, designing man.

She could not break her word to the governess, but at length, recalling the fact that she had heard Reba say her father was suspicious of Count de Lisle, she determined to repeat that to her uncle and thus put him on his guard against the villain and his probable plot to persuade Juliet into a clandestine marriage.

It was not a pleasant thing for Mildred to do. She would much rather not interfere, but Juliet must be saved at all risks. Neither she nor Reba had seemed to make a secret of their father's sentiments.

She went at once in search of Mr. Dinsmore but learned that he was closeted with a gentleman on business. Then a summons came for her to drive out with her aunt. Tea was ready when they returned, and after that she was occupied with company in the drawing room and then in assisting Juliet and Reba in dressing for the evening.

Thus the time slipped by, and when the carriage had driven away with its load of theatergoers, she retired to her own room without having had the least opportunity for a word in private with Mr. Dinsmore.

CHAPTER FIFTEENTH

It is vain
(I see) to argue 'gainst the grain.

—BUTLER

JULIET HAD SCARCELY taken her seat in Mr. Dinsmore's box when a sweeping glance around the theater showed her Count de Lisle occupying another at no great distance.

She telegraphed him behind her fan, and during the interval between the first and second acts, he joined them.

When Juliet re-entered the carriage that was to convey her home, she carried within her glove a tiny note written on fine, tinted, highly scented French paper, which he had adroitly slipped into her hand unobserved by any of her companions.

Under cover of the darkness, she transferred it to her bosom, and the first moment that she found herself alone in her dressing room, it was hastily drawn forth and read at a glance.

Her cheeks flushed and her eyes shone, and with a triumphant smile, she refolded and laid it safely by.

On leaving the room to go down to her late breakfast the next morning, she carried it with her. Not for any consideration would she have risk having it seen by other eyes than her own.

She was very late and a good deal agitated in consequence. Her thoughts were busy, too, with the important step she had determined to take that night. In her absence of mind she must have been guilty of some carelessness, for on returning to her room, after dawdling for an hour over her meal in company with her aunt and sister, she was horrified to find that the note was missing.

In vain she searched her pockets, shook out the folds of her dress, hunted everywhere, even retraced her steps all the way to the breakfast parlor and looked under and around the table.

It was hopelessly lost, and she dare not make any ado or inquiry about it.

She was exceedingly troubled but must conceal her anxiety, only hoping that it had fallen into some place where it would be undiscovered until she and the count had made good their escape from Roselands and placed themselves beyond successful pursuit.

Fortunately, as she esteemed it, no one had been witness to her perturbation or her quest, Reba and their aunt having, upon leaving the table, retired together to the boudoir of the latter.

Dire would have been Juliet's anger and alarm if she have known what had actually become of her missing treasure.

Miss Worth, in passing between the schoolroom and her own apartments, caught sight of a bit of paper lying on the floor at the head of the stairway, and stooping, picked it up.

There was neither seal nor superscription upon the outside. Thus, there seemed nothing wrong or dishonorable in opening it, for indeed how otherwise was she to learn to whom it belonged in order to restore it?

One glance told who was the writer—for she was no stranger to his peculiar chirography—to whom it was addressed, and what it signified.

"My Angel, one o'clock A.M. tomorrow. Signal, cry of an owl beneath your window. Carriage in waiting beyond the hedge.
—Your adorer"

That was all, but it needed not another word to let her, whose eyes now scanned it in indignant sorrow, fully into their plans.

She sent a quick glance around to satisfy herself that she was unseen. Then, crushing the missive in her hand, she went on her way deeply thankful that Juliet had lost it and she had found it.

Yet she was sorely perplexed and anxious. So disturbed was she that it was no easy matter to give the necessary attention to her pupils. What should she do? Appeal again to Juliet? It seemed utterly useless. But this thing must be prevented. Yes, even though it cost her the loss of her situation.

But, Harry! She shuddered and turned sick and faint at the thought that he might be taken, identified, and put on trial for the crime committed years ago. He must be saved at all risks. She would go out, meet, and warn him before he had quite reached Roselands.

He would be furious, perhaps in his rage do her some bodily harm, but—he must be saved.

She would give this note to Mr. Dinsmore, she decided, telling him where she had found it. She would tell him that she had been well-acquainted with the writer in former years and recognized the hand.

That should be sufficient to lead him to prevent Juliet's leaving the house, and if she could succeed in warning Harry away from the house, going and returning unobserved, all would be well.

But her plans miscarried. Mr. Dinsmore, as she learned on seeking an interview, had left home after an early breakfast taken hastily in his private room and would not probably return until the next day.

Here was an unexpected difficulty. What now was she to do?

She was slowly mounting the stairs in a despairing mood when a pleasant girlish voice addressed her from the hall below.

"Miss Worth, Pomp has just got back from the city with the mail, and here is a letter for you."

Mildred bounded up the stairs with the last words, put the letter into the eagerly outstretched hand of the governess, and hurried on to her own room to revel in the delights of a long epistle from her mother and sisters.

She was not half through it when there came a rap upon her door, and with brows knitting with vexation at the unwelcome interruption, she rose to open it.

She started back with an exclamation of surprise and terror as Miss Worth tottered in with a face white even to the lips and sank speechless into the nearest chair.

"What is it? What is it?" cried Mildred, hastening to bring a glass of water and hold it to her lips.

The governess swallowed a mouthful, seemingly with some difficulty, putting it aside with her hand, "Don't be alarmed," she whispered, "I shall be over it in a moment. But it was such a shock. Oh, how could he—how could he be so wicked?!"

She ended with a burst of weeping.

Mildred's sympathies were fully aroused. Laying her precious letter carefully away for future perusal, she gave herself to the task of soothing and comforting the poor distracted woman.

Miss Worth told her story brokenly, still quietly concealing the nature of the tie that connected her with the pseudo-count.

Her letter from her sister, Mrs. Marks, told of the return to America of their scoundrel brother. She said that he had paid them a hurried visit weeks ago and had gone again, they knew not where. Shortly after his departure, there had come to them a young, pretty, Italian peasant woman, who claimed to be his wife, showing proof thereof and some trinkets which they recognized as having belonged to him, a marriage certificate, and a baby boy, who was his image.

Miss Worth simply stated to Mildred the facts in regard to the note she had picked up and that her letter had brought certain intelligence that Juliet's admirer had already a living wife.

"Oh, dreadful!" cried Mildred. "Now surely you will warn her once more?"

"Yes, I will, though doubtless she will refuse to believe it of him."

"But she will not. She cannot be so infatuated as to go now and elope with him without full proof that the story of his marriage is false."

"I do not know that; she is so supremely silly. But, Miss Mildred, I must see her alone, and how am I to manage it? I have only today."

Mildred looked thoughtful. "I don't see how yet, but I must contrive to make an opportunity for you," she said. After a little more talk about ways and means, mingled with some words of sympathy and hope from the younger to the older girl, they parted, Mildred was going down to luncheon and Miss Worth to her own room.

Half an hour later Mildred joined her there with a face that told good news before she opened her lips.

"Aunt Dinsmore thinks uncle may be home tonight," she said, "and I noticed Juliet did not seem pleased to hear it. She asked how soon, and aunt said probably not before half past one or two o'clock, as the train gets into the city about midnight and he must drive over from there.

"Then aunt proposed that we four ladies should take a drive this afternoon, and Reba and I accepted her invitation at once. But Juliet declined, saying she was tired and would find more enjoyment in a novel and the sofa."

"She stays at home to make her preparations," said Miss Worth.

"Just what I think. This will be your opportunity," returned Mildred. "Is it not fortunate? Now I must go and leave you to improve it. The carriage will be at the door in a few moments."

Miss Worth sat down by her window to watch for it, and as soon as it had driven quite out of sight, she went quietly to Juliet's door and knocked.

There was no answer, though she could hear someone moving softly about the room.

She waited a moment then rapped again a little louder than before.

Still no notice was taken, the quiet footfalls and slight rustle of silken garments continuing as before.

But she persisted, repeating her knocks at short intervals and with increasing force till at length the key was turned hastily in the lock and the door thrown open, showing Juliet's fair face crimson with passion.

"Will you cease that racket?" she began, then starting back at sight of the pale determined face. "*You!*" she cried. "Is it *you*? How dare you?" And she would have slammed the door in the face of her unwelcome visitor, but Miss Worth was too quick for her, holding it forcibly open. She slipped in, pushed the door to, turned the key, and facing the girl who stood spellbound with astonishment and fury, said, "I will not apologize for my seemingly rude behavior, since you have compelled me to it. It is only for your own sake that I intrude upon you."

"Leave this room instantly!" was the passionate rejoinder. "Instantly, do you hear?" she cried, stamping her foot with rage.

"Not till I have done my errand and cleared my skirts of your ruin, if you are still so infatuated as to rush upon it," returned the governess quietly, folding her arms and placing her back against the door.

"I have already told you that the man who seeks your hand is a deceiver—a spurious nobleman, a mere fortune hunter—"

"Stop!" cried Juliet, interrupting her with fury and again stamping her foot. "Stop! And leave this room, or I will summon the servants to put you out."

"No, you will not do that," Miss Worth returned with a contemptuous smile. "You will not want them to hear what I have to tell of your adorer, or rather the adorer of your wealth. I will not go till I have finished what I came to say."

"You think to rob me of him," sneered Juliet, "but you are mistaken. You are too old and ugly. If he ever fancied you, it is all past; he can never do so again. But I can't believe that you were ever really pretty, for you are as ugly as sin now."

"Thank you," the governess answered with irony. "I rejoice to learn that you think sin ugly, for it is sin for you to allow this man to play the lover to you. And it would be a dreadful sin to marry him—not only because of the entire disapproval of your parents, but," she added with strong emphasis, "because he *already has a wife.*"

For a moment Juliet was struck dumb with astonishment. But, recovering herself, "I don't believe it!" she cried, her cheek crimsoning and her eyes flashing. "I don't believe a word of it. And if I did, I'd marry him all the same," she added, grinding her teeth. "I would, for I love him! I love him! And you needn't tell me he's a villain!"

"Marry him! The ceremony would be a mere farce, and you a—not a wife, for you could not be that while his lawful, wedded wife still lives."

Miss Worth spoke with slow distinctness, her eyes fixed severely upon Juliet's face.

The latter started back as if stung. Then, resuming her haughty, defiant air, "How dare you!" she repeated. "What is he to you? And what proof can you bring of all that you assert against him?"

"What he is to me does not concern you," said Miss Worth. "My knowledge of his marriage was gained today by a letter from his sister, but if I show it to you, you would of course ask how you were to know that he was the man referred to or that she was a reliable witness. No, I can prove nothing, but if you are wise, you will require proof that he is a man who has a right to offer you his hand, who can make you his lawful wife, and who to marry will not be ruin."

"Then, I am not wise. Now, go!"

"I obey you since my errand is now done," returned the governess with a stately bow as she unlocked the door and threw it wide open.

Stepping into the hall, she faced her antagonist again for an instant. "If you will persist in this madness, on your own head be your ruin. My skirts are clear," she said and swept proudly away.

It cost Mildred quite an effort to give due attention to Reba's chatter and the small talk of her aunt during the hour or more of their drive. Her thoughts were very full of the interview then in progress between Miss Worth and Juliet.

On reaching home, she repaired directly to the room of the former to hear an account of it.

This the governess gave in detail, concluding with, "You see, Miss Keith, it is just as I expected. She will not hear reason; she will take no warning. She is fully bent upon carrying out this mad act, and if we save her, it will be in spite of herself."

"Yes, and we have but little time to consider how we shall do it," said Mildred. "What is your plan?"

"To go myself, a little before his appointed hour, to meet and warn him away, while you remain in the house and on watch to prevent her from leaving it to join him. Are you willing to undertake that, Miss Mildred?"

"Yes, to the best of my ability. I will rouse the whole house if necessary to prevent her from getting away with him."

"Thank you," Miss Worth said earnestly. "Miss Keith, I am very sorry to have to call upon you for this assistance, for it will involve the loss of your night's rest. But Mr. Dinsmore being unfortunately away—"

"Don't speak of it," interrupted Mildred rather impulsively. "It is a very small sacrifice on my part, for I am well and pretty strong again, but you look wretchedly ill."

"Never mind me. I shall be better when this is over," Miss Worth answered with a faint smile.

"I will leave you to lie down and rest," Mildred said, rising to go. "Can't you sleep through the early part of the night, if I am on guard and ready to wake you at midnight?"

The governess shook her head. "I cannot sleep till this is over, but it will tend to dull Juliet's suspicions if you will retire at your usual hour and let me call you when the appointed hour draws near."

"It is a wise thought, and we will do so," said Mildred. "And now I must go and dress for dinner. Try not to be so very anxious. I do believe it will turn out well," she added hopefully as she left the room.

CHAPTER SIXTEENTH

Muse not that I thus suddenly proceed;
For what I will, I will, and there's an end.

—SHAKESPEARE

THERE WERE GUESTS from the neighborhood at both dinner and tea, some of whom remained during the evening.

Juliet was unusually happy and sprightly, but to Mildred, who watched her furtively, her unwonted mirthfulness seemed to cover other and deeper feelings. There were signs of agitation, perhaps unnoticed by a casual observer—a nervous tremor, a hectic flush on her cheek, a slight start at some sudden noise or an unexpected address.

She was thrumming on the piano and shrieking out an air from a popular opera at the top of her voice when, at ten o'clock, Mildred slipped quietly away to her own room.

Merely exchanging her evening dress for a neat dressing gown, Mildred threw herself upon a couch to await Miss Worth's summons, and contrary to her expectations, she presently fell sound asleep.

She was awakened by a touch on the shoulder and started up to find the governess standing by her side.

"Will you come now, Miss Keith?" she asked in low, agitated tones. "It is half past twelve, and I must start out at once."

"Yes, I am quite ready," Mildred answered, and wrapping a shawl about her shoulders, she followed the lead of the governess.

A window on the landing of the principal staircase, down which Juliet would be likely to pass, was on the same side of the house with the one under which the signal was to be given.

There could be no better post of observation, and here Mildred seated herself upon the broad sill, while her companion, parting from her with a whispered word of mingled thanks, caution, and entreaty, glided down the stairs and let herself out at a side door, using extreme caution to make no noise.

Thence she gained the avenue and beyond that the road. Here she paused and hesitated. She was not sure from which direction her brother would come; but she must make a choice.

She did so and crept onward, keeping to a narrow footpath that ran parallel to the road and between it and a hedge that enclosed the lawn and orchard.

Left thus alone, Mildred sat still, her heart beating fast with excitement and timidity, for the house was dark and silent almost as a grave.

But she thought of Him to whom the night shineth as the day and darkness and light are both alike, and with that thought, she grew calm and quiet. She was in the path of duty, and she need fear no evil, because He was with her.

Yet, the waiting time seemed long. How would it

end? If Miss Worth were successful, only in her stealthy return; otherwise, probably with the signal and then a struggle between Juliet and herself.

She had begun to breathe more freely with the thought that the time for that had passed, and she was straining her ear to catch the faint sound of Miss Worth's approach when the loud hoot of an owl from the shrubbery beneath the window broke the silence with a suddenness that nearly startled her from her seat and set her heart to throbbing wildly again.

She pressed her hand against her side to still it, while she bent forward, listening intently for some answering sound from above.

There was a moment of utter stillness, then a slight creak, as of a door opened with extreme care, followed by other slight sounds, as though someone were stealing softly down the hall. Mildred slipped from her perch and back into the shadow of the wall, almost holding her breath for what was to come.

The stealthy step drew nearer. Something was gliding past her when, with a quick movement, she stepped before and threw her arms around it — a tall, slight figure muffled in a cloak.

There was a low, half-stifled cry and a struggle for release.

"Unhand me," muttered Juliet in a tone of intense, suppressed fury. "Is there no limit to your insolent interference?"

"Juliet, it is I!" whispered Mildred, not relaxing her hold in the least. "I only want to save you from falling prey to a villain who is only after your money and would ruin you to get it. He already has a wife."

"I don't believe a word of it! Let me go, let me go, I say!" Wrenching herself free, she dealt Mildred a blow that sent her staggering against the wall.

But she recovered herself instantly and sprang after Juliet, who was gliding down the stairs toward the lower hall.

She caught her, as they reached the hall below.

"Juliet, Juliet, are you mad?" she panted. "Will you forsake all you love—all that life holds dear for that scoundrel?"

"What business is it of yours?" demanded Juliet fiercely, trying with all her strength to shake her off. "I tell you I will not be prevented by you or anybody. Let go of me, I say, or I will do you a mischief."

"I will not let you go," returned Mildred. "Come back, or I will call aloud and rouse the house." What would have happened it is impossible to tell, had not help come at that precise moment.

A carriage had driven up to the front entrance, the rumble of its wheels sending the cowardly villain in the shrubbery flying to the adjacent woods.

The girls, in the excitement of their struggle, had not heard its approach, but the sudden opening of the front door and the sound of Mr. Dinsmore's step and voice as he entered accompanied by his servant, to whom he was giving some order as to the disposal of his luggage, caused them to loose their hold of each other.

Juliet fairly flew up the stairs, while Mildred dropped into a chair, her strength completely forsaking her with the sudden withdrawal of the necessity for its exertion.

"Who is there?" demanded Mr. Dinsmore, his ear catching the rustle of Juliet's garments and the sounds of Mildred's heavy breathing.

"Solon, strike a light instantly."

"It is I, uncle," panted Mildred, bursting into hysterical sobs.

"You, Mildred!" he exclaimed in utter astonishment as he recognized the voice. "Why, child, what on earth are you doing here at this time of night? All in the dark, too. What has gone wrong? Are you ill?"

Solon had struck a match and succeeded in lighting the hall lamp. With Mr. Dinsmore's last question, its rays fell full upon Mildred's face, showing it pale, agitated, and with eyes brimming with tears.

"Why, you are as white as a sheet!" he exclaimed, laying his hand affectionately on her shoulder. "Child, child, what is the matter?"

In a few rapid, rather incoherent sentences, she gave him an inkling of the state of affairs, to which he returned a volley of questions without waiting for an answer to any of them. "Out into the shrubbery, Solon," he commanded, "call Ajax and Pomp to help. Catch the rascal if you can and bring him to me."

Then to Mildred, repeating his queries, "Where is Juliet?" he asked. "Where is Miss Worth? How does she come to know the villain or his plot to carry off Juliet? What is he to her?"

"I don't know, sir, what he is to Miss Worth," said Mildred, "but she says she has known him all his life, and a letter she received today told her of his marriage—that he has a living wife."

"He has? The scoundrel!" cried her listener.

"Yes, sir, and of course, on learning that, Miss Worth was more than ever determined to frustrate his plans."

"Well, what more, and where is this precious fool of a Juliet? I wish all girls were blessed with your common sense, child."

"She ran upstairs as you came in, sir."

"And may have come down by the back stairway and made off with the rascal, after all!" he exclaimed in alarm. "Run up to her room, Milly, and see if she is there, while I look about below here."

Mildred went at once, though she would much rather have been excused, for the errand was no pleasant one. She was reluctant to meet Juliet again at that moment but fortunately was spared the necessity, for on nearing the door of Juliet's sleeping room, she distinctly heard her voice in conversation with Reba.

She hurried down again with her report, which her uncle received with grim satisfaction.

"That is well," he said. "Now I'll join in the search for the scoundrel, and I promise you that if we catch him, he'll not get away unhurt. But where is Miss Worth, child? You have not answered that question yet."

As he spoke, a side door opened, and a tall, black-robed figure glided in.

"Miss Worth!" he exclaimed, catching sight of her face.

"Yes," she said in a hoarse whisper, leaning back against the wall and looking ready to faint.

"You are ill," he said. "Let me help you into the library and give you a glass of wine."

She hardly seemed to hear him at all. Her eyes were fixed in eager, terrified questioning upon Mildred's face.

"Juliet is in her room," the latter hastened to say.

"Thank God for that!" she said in quivering tones. "And he?"

"Is gone I suppose. No one has seen him, as far as I know."

At that moment, one of the men put his head in at the door. "Can't find the rascal, massa. I reckon he dun gone cl'ar off de place."

"Quite likely, but as he may return. You are to be on the watch till sunrise," was the reply.

"You didn't meet him?" Mildred ask, drawing near the governess and speaking in an undertone.

"No, I must have taken the wrong road. Mr. Dinsmore, I owe you an explanation. Shall it be given now?"

The voice was very low, very tremulous, but the sad eyes were lifted unflinchingly to his stern face.

"As you please," he said, his features softening a little at sight of her distress. "You look hardly able to make it now, and some hours later will answer just as well. Indeed, I think we would all do well to go to our beds as soon as possible. But stay a moment."

He stepped into the dining room and returned with a glass of wine, which he offered to the governess, saying, "You look ready to faint. Drink this; it will do you good."

"No, no, never!" she cried, shuddering and recoiling as from a serpent. "It has been the ruin of those I love best."

"Very well," he said rather coldly. "Mildred, will you take it?"

"No, thank you, uncle. I do not need it and would rather not," the young girl answered pleasantly.

"Silly girl," he said, draining the glass himself. "Well, good night, ladies, or rather good morning. Miss Worth, I will see you in the library directly after breakfast."

So saying, he left them.

"What a blessing that it has turned out so well," Mildred said to her companion.

"Has it?" asked the governess in a bewildered tone, putting her hand to her head. "I feel as though the earth were reeling beneath my feet. I cannot think."

"Let me help you to your room. A few hours' rest will make all right again with you, I trust," Mildred said compassionately.

"Don't allow yourself to feel at all anxious or distressed," she went on, as she assisted her up the stairs. "I am sure uncle will not be hard with you when he learns how free from blame you are. Juliet has been saved, and he seems to have escaped and will not be likely to try it again."

"Ah, if I could have met and warned him," sighed the governess.

"Surely it is better as it is, since he got away without," reasoned Mildred, "for might he not have been angry and abusive?"

"True, too true!" she murmured, catching at the balusters to keep from falling. "Yes, it is better so, but my brain reels and I cannot think."

Mildred was alarmed. "What can I do for you?" she asked.

"Nothing, nothing, but help me to my bed, thank you. I shall be better when I have slept off this horrible fatigue and weakness. Oh, such a tramp and weary waiting as it was—out in the cold and darkness on a lonely road!" she gasped shudderingly, as she sank down upon her bed. "It seemed as if I should drop down and die before I could get back to the house. And my terror for him! That was the worst of all!"

"I don't think he deserves your love and care for him!" Mildred said, her indignation waxing hot against the worthless villain.

"Perhaps not," she sighed, "but he cared for me once, and he was a noble fellow then. And I—ah, he told me I had helped to ruin him!"

"But it wasn't true?" Mildred said in a tone of indignant inquiry.

Miss Worth did not seem to hear. "I shall go now," she said presently. "You need rest. Do go to your bed, Miss Mildred. Perhaps I shall sleep if left alone."

Perceiving that she could be of no further assistance, Mildred went not unwillingly, for she, too, was quite worn out with fatigue and excitement.

It was eight o'clock when she awoke, but she was ready for the summons to breakfast, which was not served that morning until nearly nine.

Juliet did not make an appearance at the meal. She was indisposed, Reba reported, and she would take a cup of tea in her own room.

"That is the best place for her," commented Mr. Dinsmore shortly.

"What do you mean by that?" queried his wife, who had heard nothing of the events of the past night.

"Just what I say, and I hope she will have the grace to stay there till her father comes for her, as I requested him to do by this morning's mail."

"Mr. Dinsmore, *will* you please explain yourself?" exclaimed his wife in a tone of exasperation.

"It will not require many words," he answered dryly. "She would have eloped with another woman's husband last night if she had not been hindered."

"Another woman's husband!" echoed Reba in astonishment and dismay. "I did not know it was so bad as that!"

"Dreadful! Impossible!" cried Mrs. Dinsmore, dropping her knife and fork and bursting into tears. "Don't tell me a niece of mine could do such a thing as that! Mr. Dinsmore, it's a cruel joke."

"No joke at all," he said, "but the simple and unvarnished truth. Though, of course, she refused to believe that the man was married."

"Who is the wretch?" cried his wife, grinding her teeth. "If you'd been a man, you'd have shot him down!"

"I'm no murderer, madam," was the biting retort, "and in my opinion a whipping would much better befit so cowardly a scoundrel. I should have administered that with hearty good will, could I have laid hands on him."

"I wish you had!" she exclaimed with vehemence. "I am glad you wrote for Mr. Marsden, and I hope he will come at once and take that shameful girl away before she does anything more to bring disgrace on this family. Reba, why did you let her do so?"

"I, Aunt Belle? I'm not in her confidence and was as ignorant and innocent as yourself in regard to the whole thing."

"Who did hinder her? Am I not to hear the whole story?" demanded Mrs. Dinsmore, turning to her spouse again.

"I presume it will all be unfolded to you in time," was the cool reply. "I have not heard it fully myself yet. Mildred here," he said, looking pleasantly at her, "knows more about it than I do, and to her, I believe, our thanks are due for preventing the mischief."

"To Miss Worth, uncle, much more than to me," Mildred said, blushing and feeling decidedly uncomfortable under the surprised, scrutinizing glances of her aunt and Reba. "It was she who found it out, tried to persuade Juliet to give it up, and when she failed in that, told me—"

"Told you!" interrupted Mrs. Dinsmore with great indignation. "Why did she not come to me instead? I was the proper person by all odds."

Mildred was at a loss for a reply that should not damage the cause of the governess, but Mr. Dinsmore came to her relief. "I presume, my dear, it was to save you from the mortification of hearing of your niece's contemplated folly, and her from that of having made you acquainted with it."

CHAPTER SEVENTEENTH

Do not insult calamity:
It is a barbarous grossness to lay on
The weight of scorn, when heavy misery
Too much already weighs men's fortunes down.

—DANIEL

RETURNING TO HER room to don her riding habit directly after breakfast, Mildred met Miss Worth on her way to the library to keep her appointment with Mr. Dinsmore.

"How pale and ill you look!" exclaimed Mildred.

"Ah, you would not wonder if you knew how I shrink from this interview," sighed the governess.

"I think you need not," Mildred answered kindly. Then she gave her the substance of the conversation at the table in regard to the past night's occurrences, adding that her uncle's explanation of her probable motives had entirely appeased Mrs. Dinsmore's anger and that presumably he did not himself hold her in great disfavor.

"How very good of you to tell me, Miss Keith," the governess said, grateful tears springing to her eyes. "But I must not delay another moment, lest I keep him waiting."

She hastened on into the library and was relieved to find it tenantless. Unpunctuality would not have helped her cause, and though the moments of waiting tried her already overstrained nerves, she was thankful that they had fallen to her lot rather than to his.

She had slept little, waking early and not greatly refreshed, and she was tormented with anxiety in regard to her brother's whereabouts, likelihood to renew his attempt to carry off Juliet, and danger of arrest on the old charges. This in addition to the care that came upon her every day—the ever-recurring question of how she was to meet necessary expenses for herself and those dependent upon her.

Almost too weary to stand, yet too restless to remain quiet, she dropped into a chair for a moment. Then she rose and paced the floor, at last pausing beside the fire and standing there with her right elbow on the mantel, her forehead in the open palm of her hand, and her eyes cast down while painful thought surged through her brain.

Thus Mr. Dinsmore found her, so absorbed in her meditations that she was not even aware of his entrance until he coughed slightly to attract her attention. Then she came out of her reverie with a start.

"Excuse me, sir, but I was not aware that I was no longer alone."

"Time enough," he said. "And let me compliment you on being more punctual than myself. But you are not looking well or happy."

"No, sir, and I think you will hardly wonder that I do not, when you have heard what I am here to tell."

"Be seated," he said, waving his hand toward an easy chair while taking possession of its fellow. "Let me hear what it is."

She seemed at a loss where to begin her story, and to help her, he remarked interrogatively, "I presume you have no objection to explaining the cause of your mysterious nocturnal ramble?"

"No," she said, "I went to warn that man away from the house."

"Ah! yes. That may have been the better plan, as I was absent from home, but what puzzles me is to understand how you knew of his coming."

"I had picked this up in the hall," she said, handing him the little note.

"But how could it tell you so much, since it gives neither the name of the writer nor that of the person addressed?"

"The man's writing is perfectly familiar to me," she explained, growing a shade paler as she spoke. "I have known him intimately for years and had learned from him his designs upon Miss Marsden."

"An intimate acquaintance of yours!" he exclaimed in astonishment. "Not one to be proud of, certainly. May I ask a further explanation? It is a matter of some consequence to know with what style of persons the instructress of my children associates."

"I know it. You have a perfect right to ask," she stammered, a crimson blush suffusing her cheek and hot tears rushing into the downcast eyes. "Oh, may you never know, Mr. Dinsmore, what it is to have those nearest and dearest bring shame and disgrace upon you!"

"A relative?" he asked. "Is he not a foreigner?"

She shook her head sorrowfully, and after a moment's struggle for composure, she told him what the man was to her, how he had been led astray by love of the wine cup and the evil influence of an older villain. She told how he had left his country years ago, traveling his family knew not where, and how unexpectedly she had recognized him as the pseudo-Count of whom Juliet had become enamored. She told how she had entreated him to go away, and failing to persuade him, how she had made a fruitless appeal to Juliet, disclosing his real character and aims, only to be condemned as an envious rival. Then she told how she had sought himself with the purpose of calling in his aid to save the willful girl from the destruction she courted, and failing to find him at home, had enlisted Mildred in the cause.

"Miss Juliet Marsden is a born simpleton!" he commented impatiently. "Well, Miss Worth, she owes a great deal to your good sense and right feeling. I, too, am obliged to you. I sympathize with you in the trial of having such a brother, and I do not see that you have been at all to blame in this unfortunate matter but rather the contrary.

"However, Mrs. Dinsmore is not always entirely reasonable in her views and requirements, and it is altogether likely she would object to receiving your services as governess to her children, if she knew of your relationship to this man. We will, therefore, keep that matter to ourselves."

So saying, he dismissed her and the subject

together with a wave of his hand, and she withdrew with one burden somewhat lightened.

For some days, nothing special occurred at Roselands. Juliet kept to her own apartments, for the most part alone or with no companionship but that of her maid. Reba's strongly expressed disgust and indignation at her folly had sent Juliet into a fit of the pouts, so that they had small relish for each other's society. Mrs. Dinsmore, angry with her neice for the disgrace she had so nearly brought upon the family, would not go near her nor allow any of the children to do so.

Mildred, too, stayed away, partly in obedience to a hint from her aunt and partly because she did not suppose her company would be acceptable, she and Juliet having never been kindred spirits.

Meanwhile, Miss Worth still took her meals in the nursery with the younger children, doing so of choice. She attended faithfully to her duties in the schoolroom but was seldom seen at other times. Her light often burned far into the night, and day by day she grew thinner and paler, her cheeks more sunken, her eyes more hollow, and her step slower and more languid.

Mildred alone seemed to note the change, but to her kind inquiries the governess always answered that she was well in a tone that did not encourage further inquiry or remark.

Mr. Marsden was slow in responding to Mr. Dinsmore's summons, but at length a letter was received, announcing his intention of starting on his journey two days after the date of his letter and requesting Mr. Dinsmore to keep a vigilant watch over Juliet until his arrival.

It had come by the mail, which, arriving in the city the previous night, was brought to Roselands by Pomp in the morning.

Mr. Dinsmore opened it at the breakfast table, read it to himself, and with a satisfied smile, passed it on to his wife for her perusal while he opened the newspaper and leisurely glanced over its contents.

"Ah! he exclaimed presently with some excitement, "here is a bit of news. Listen!"

He read it aloud:

"'Yesterday, a gentleman from Philadelphia, visiting in our city, met in the street and recognized an old acquaintance, one Henry Worth, formerly of Philadelphia, who, some five years ago, fled thence to escape trial on a charge of forgery.

"'Worth was from a respectable family; his father had been a man of very considerable wealth but had failed shortly before the commission of the crime — brought to ruin, it is said, by the excesses of this son.

"'The young man has been leading a merry life of late in the assumed character of a French nobleman — calling himself the Count de Lisle. The gentleman referred to above promptly reported his case to the police. Worth was arrested and is now safely lodged in prison, whence he will be sent north in a few days for trial.'"

"So it's all true — that he was a scoundrel!" cried Mrs. Dinsmore. "His name's Worth! He's Miss Worth's brother! I know it! I'm sure of it! That accounts for her knowing all about him. What a wicked, deceitful thing to hide it as she has done and impose herself—the sister of a convict—on me as governess to my children! I never heard anything so shameful! I'll give her notice at once, and—"

"Why, my dear, what absurd folly!" exclaimed Mr. Dinsmore impatiently, angry with her for her unreasonable displeasure and with himself for having inadvertently read out the name. "What difference does it make?"

"What difference, Mr. Dinsmore? Are you crazy? You may consider paupers and convicts proper associates for your children, but they are not for mine. That woman shall go."

"She is neither a pauper nor a convict," he said, "nor in the least responsible, so far as I have been able to learn, for the wrongdoing of this man, whom, by the way, you do not know to be her brother. And even if he is, I should think a woman's heart would feel for her in the terrible sorrow and disgrace of having such a relative."

"Papa, what is a convict?" asked Lora.

"One legally proved guilty of a crime," he said. "And, my dear, the term does not yet apply to the man himself—much less to your governess—as he has not yet been brought to trial."

"It's all the same," Mrs. Dinsmore sneered, "for I haven't a doubt of his guilt. There, you needn't smile as if I had said a foolish thing!"

"I wish you would not *do* a foolish thing and send away one so well-qualified for her duties and faithful in their performance as Miss Worth, merely because she is so unfortunate as to bear the same name—possibly be nearly related to—a scamp."

"Dear me, papa, I think mamma is quite right," remarked Louise with a toss of her head. "I'm sure I don't wish to be taught by such a person."

"When your opinion is desired, Louise, it will be called for," said her father severely. "In the meantime, you may reserve it."

"Well, I mean to ask Miss Worth if that man is her brother!" muttered the child sullenly.

"You will do no such thing!" returned her father. "I will not have a word said to her about it."

At that, his wife smiled significantly.

"It might be as well to show that paragraph to Juliet," she said, rising from the table. "Suppose you give me the paper."

"Do so, by all means," he replied, handing it to her.

"Mildred, here is something for Miss Worth. Will you see that she gets it?"

It, too, was a newspaper, and Mildred hoped compassionately, as she carried it up the stairs, that it did not contain the item of distressing news for Miss Worth that Mr. Dinsmore had read from the other.

Mrs. Dinsmore had preceded her by several minutes, and her voice, speaking in cold, cutting tones, came to the girl's ear from the upper hall, as she set foot upon the first stair.

"You must be aware that your services are no longer acceptable here," she was saying. "In fact, you would never have been given the situation had I known of this disgraceful connection. I must say I am justly indignant at the gross deception that has been practiced upon me."

"She must be speaking to Miss Worth. Oh, what cruel words!" thought Mildred.

"She had reached the landing, and turning to ascend the short flight above, she caught sight of the speaker and the person addressed.

Miss Worth stood leaning against the wall, one hand clutching at the balustrade for support. Her face was deathly pale, and her lips were trembling. Mrs. Dinsmore stood a few feet from her, gathering her dainty skirts close to her person as if fearful of contamination, her aristocratic nose held high in the air, her countenance expressing scorn, contempt, and righteous indignation.

"What have you to say for yourself, Miss Worth?" she demanded.

"Nothing but that I am guiltless of any intentional wrong," the governess replied, lifting her head and speaking in a tone of quiet despair. "I have faithfully performed my duties as your governess to the best of my ability."

"You don't deny, then, that this scoundrel, that this felon—"

"Madame," interrupted the governess, her eyes flashing while a bright red spot burned on each cheek. "He is not that, for he has never been convicted of, nor so much as brought to trial for, any crime."

"Insolence!" exclaimed Mrs. Dinsmore. "Well, if he hasn't been yet, he soon will be and get his deserts, I sincerely hope."

And picking up the newspaper, which seemed to have dropped from Miss Worth's nerveless hand, she swept on toward Juliet's apartments. In another moment, she had disappeared within them, shutting the door after her.

The fire had died out of Miss Worth's eye. The red had left her cheek, and she was swaying from side to side, only her hold on the balustrade keeping her from falling.

Mildred sprang toward her. "Lean on me," she said. "Let me help you to your room. Don't be so troubled. The Lord will take care of you and yours, if you put your trust in Him."

She did not know whether or not her words were heard or understood. The poor woman answered only with a heavy sigh and whispered, "Thank you. I shall be better soon. But oh, what will become of them all? My mother, my poor mother! He was her pride, her idol!"

Sympathetic tears streamed over Mildred's cheeks as she assisted her to her room.

"I'm to go away, Miss Mildred," she said. "I'll be turned out in disgrace for what is no fault of mine — no fault but my bitter, bitter sorrow! God help me and those dependent on me!"

"He will," Mildred answered chokingly. "He is so kind, so full of compassion; His tender mercies are over all His works!"

She stayed a little while, trying to administer consolation. Then, putting the paper into Miss Worth's hands, merely saying that it had come by the morning's mail, she went away.

Finding Rachel busy in her room, she stepped back into the hall and stood for a few moments at the window there, looking out into the avenue below, where Mr. Dinsmore was mounting his horse to make his daily morning round of the plantation.

Suddenly, there was a sound in Miss Worth's room as of a heavy body falling to the floor.

Mildred ran to her door, rushing in without the ceremony of knocking, and found the poor governess stretched, apparently lifeless, upon the floor, the newspaper lying by her side.

Her eye, as she stooped over the prostrate form, was caught by a paragraph that was heavily marked.

But the present was no time to examine it, and pushing the paper aside, she hastened to loosen the clothing of the fainting woman. At the same time, she give directions to the two or three servants who had been attracted by the noise of the fall and had followed her into the room.

"Throw open that window, Minerva! Some cold water, Fanny, quick, quick! And you, Rachel, run to my room for my smelling salts."

"Oh, Miss Milly, is she done gone dead?" asked Fanny fearfully as she sprinkled the water upon the still, white face.

"No, no, it's only a bad faint," Mildred answered, but her own heart quaked with fear as she spoke. The pinched features of the governess' face were so deathlike in their fixedness and pallor, and in spite of every effort, they remained so till, nearly wild with terror, Mildred bade the servants summon other assistance.

"Call Mrs. Brown," she said. "Ask aunt if we shall not send for the doctor."

They hurried away to do her bidding while she renewed her exertions, sending up silent, importunate petitions all the while to her heavenly Friend.

They were answered. Miss Worth sighed deeply, opened her eyes, and lifted them to the young face bent over her with a look of such hopeless, heartbreaking anguish that the girl at once burst into sobs and tears.

"Oh, what is it? What is it?" she said.

"He—he was my husband—and—and I *loved him*," came a hoarse whisper from the colorless lips, and with the last word, she swooned again.

"She has lost her reason," thought Mildred. "Poor, poor thing! Oh, perhaps it may be better for her if she never comes to herself again."

CHAPTER EIGHTEENTH

Never morning wore
To evening,
but some heart did break.

—TENNYSON

THEY BROUGHT THE housekeeper and the family physician. The latter pronounced the patient very ill and with good reason, for she passed out of one swoon only to fall into another, till they thought that her end was surely near at hand.

However, after some hours, the immediate danger seemed over, and the doctor left, promising to return before night.

Mrs. Dinsmore had been awed and frightened into something slightly akin to terror and remorse on account of her excessive harshness, but now she shook it off.

"Really, she takes her dismissal very hard," she remarked to Mildred as the latter was leaving the dinner table. "I had no idea she was so much attached to Roselands."

"I do not think it could be that alone, aunt," Mildred returned in surprise and disgust.

"What then?"

"Her relative's disgrace and the poverty and distress to herself and a mother and sister dependent on her, consequent on her being thrown out of gainful employment."

Then with a sudden recollection of that paper with its marked paragraph, Mildred hastened from the room and went in search of it.

The patient had fallen asleep, Rachel watching at her side.

A glance showed Mildred the paper folded and laid upon the table. She opened it cautiously, found the article she sought, and read it.

A case of lynching occurred in one of the most southern counties of Texas about two weeks ago. A man named Joseph White, said to be from one of the Northern States, was suspected of horse stealing and was taken by a posse of some forty armed men, carried into the woods, and hung. He was given ten minutes to prepare for death and died bravely, protesting his innocence to the last, but, of course, nobody believed him, as the proof against him was strong.

Sick and faint with horror, Mildred laid down the paper and dropped shuddering into a chair. Oh, this was worse than all! If he was that poor woman's husband, and she loved him, no wonder news so dreadful, and coming at such a time as this, should bring her down to the very gates of death.

Mildred's girlish heart was filled with a great compassion for the poor stricken creature, a great longing to comfort her in her grief and desolation.

"She will not live, she cannot," she whispered to herself. "I should not wish to live were I in her place. It is so horrible, so horrible! How can men be such savages as to take human life to atone for the loss of an animal, and that perhaps the life of an innocent man?"

"I should be loath to assume your responsibility in this matter," remarked Mr. Dinsmore to his wife as Mildred left them lingering over their dessert.

"Why?" she demanded, bridling. "Did I cause the ruin of her brother or the poverty of the family?"

"You seem to have added to that last burden by your dismissal, thus supplying the one drop that makes the cup overflow."

"I was only doing my duty to my children," she retorted angrily.

"I cannot see it," he said. "The children have improved very much in the two years that she has been with us."

"And, of course, all the credit for that belongs to her! There is none at all due to me. I often wonder, Mr. Dinsmore, how you came to marry a woman for whom you entertain so little admiration or respect."

"That is hardly a fair inference from what I have said," he rejoined in a tone of weariness and disgust. She had tried his patience not a little that day with her whims and follies.

He rose with the last word and withdrew to the library. He was sitting before the fire in his easy chair, seemingly lost in thought, when the door opened softly and Mildred glided across the room and stood at his side.

As he looked up, he saw that her features were working with emotion and her eyes were full of tears.

"What is it?" he asked in a startled tone. "She's not gone, I hope?"

Mildred shook her head and with a burst of tears and a whispered, "I could almost wish she was if—if I was quite sure she was prepared," pointed significantly to the marked paragraph in the paper which she held before him.

He read it and then looked up at her with an inquiring "Well?" upon which Mildred told her reasons for connecting that item of news with Miss Worth's sudden seizure, repeating the words gasped out by the pale, trembling lips of the governess on her partial restoration to consciousness.

"I thought then that her mind wandered," concluded Mildred, "but since reading this, I fear her words were only too true."

"Poor thing!" he sighed. "I'm afraid she knows by sad experience all that she rescued Juliet from. Well, Milly, we will do the best we can for her. And, child, don't distress yourself unnecessarily. It will do her no good, you know."

"You are always kind and thoughtful of me, uncle," she responded gratefully, "but this seems no time to be considering myself. Do you know what the doctor thinks of her?"

"He said that he thought her attack must have been occasioned by some severe mental shock coming upon an exhausted frame. What she has had to exhaust her I don't know—her duties were light enough, I supposed—but the shock I took to have been the arrest of her brother. It would seem, however, from this, that a far more terrible one was heaped upon the other."

"Yes," Mildred said, shuddering. "Oh, my heart bleeds for her. But how strange that she is married. Why should she have kept it so profound a secret, going back to her maiden name?

"That I cannot tell," Mr. Dinsmore answered, "but probably it was a clandestine and unfortunate affair, and she wished to avoid unpleasant explanations. We shall say nothing to your aunt, as it would only increase her displeasure against the unhappy woman."

"Ah, uncle," Mildred said musingly, "how little idea I have had hitherto of the dreadful distress that comes into some lives! I begin to think myself a very fortunate mortal."

"It is well to learn to appreciate our blessings," he returned with a smile that had little mirth in it, for he was thinking with concern of the condition and prospects of the stranger within his gates.

"I must ask Dr. Barton whether she is likely to be long ill," he said, thinking aloud rather than addressing Mildred, "that we may make arrangements accordingly. And I think we should show him this," indicating the fatal news item.

"But it is her secret," Mildred said doubtfully.

"True, my dear, but physicians often have to be entrusted with the secrets of their patients, and Dr. Barton is a safe depository for such things.

Mrs. Dinsmore was impatient for Dr. Barton's opinion, very impatient over the unfortunate circumstances of the serious seizure of the governess under her roof, for she entertained an utter detestation of sickness and death and was always ready to fly from them at a moment's warning. Whatever might be the character of the illness, she insisted there was danger of contagion and saw it to be clearly her duty to take care of herself and her children by running away.

She spent the afternoon in overseeing the packing of trunks so she might be prepared for a hasty exit, then anxiously awaited the doctor's report.

It was her husband who brought it to her at last, late in the evening. He had been closeted for a quarter of an hour with the physician and now came into his wife's boudoir with a countenance full of grave concern.

"Well, what is it? What do does Dr. Barton say?" she queried fretfully, "I thought you would never come back to tell me."

"He fears there is little hope of recovery," her husband answered gravely, pacing slowly to and fro with the air of one who is seriously disturbed.

"And is she going to be sick long?"

"It may be for some weeks. He cannot tell with certainty."

"Can she be moved?"

"Moved? What occasion for that? The room she occupies now is comfortable, is it not?"

"Dear me, Mr. Dinsmore, you can be very stupid! I want to know if she can't be sent to the village to a hotel or boarding house. It isn't at all pleasant to think of her dying here. I don't want any haunted rooms in my house."

He paused in his walk and stood looking at her in amazement that presently gave way to an expression of extreme chagrin and disgust.

"Isabella!" he exclaimed. "Are you completely and utterly heartless? Are you utterly destitute of womanly compassion for the helpless and suffering?"

"Of course I'm not," she said, resorting to tears, as was her wont when at a loss for better weapons of defense. "I'm sure she could be made very comfortable there and I spared the necessity of being turned out of my own home in the depth of winter. But you can think of everybody's comfort and happiness except your wife's—*it* isn't of the least consequence and never will be."

"Really," he said, "I do not know what you are talking about. I certainly have not proposed your leaving home and cannot see the slightest necessity for your doing so."

"No, you would be quite well pleased to have me stay here and get sick and die. That would give you a chance to find a younger and prettier wife."

He disdained a reply to that, and presently she went on: "I shall take the children and go to Kentucky to visit my sister. It's fortunate that Mr. Marsden comes tomorrow and is going to return immediately. I could not have a better escort."

"As you please. I have become somewhat used to being left out of my wife's plans," he said coldly, turning on his heel to leave the room. "Go, if you like," he added, turning toward her again. "But don't talk of necessity, for there is not the remotest danger of Miss Worth's sickness proving contagious. She is dying of a broken heart."

"Ridiculous!" Mrs. Dinsmore muttered as her husband went out and closed the door. "The idea of a governess coming to such a romantic end—it's far more likely to turn out to be scarlet fever or smallpox."

By morning, she had worked herself up to the belief that such was really the case.

The next step was to bring her nieces to a like conviction, in which she succeeded so well that they were greatly alarmed. Juliet nearly forgot the disappointment and disgrace of her late attempt at elopement in the fear that smallpox might rob her of her beauty.

She had not much to lose, to be sure, but of that fact she was comfortably ignorant. What beauty she had was but skin deep, and smallpox would have made sad havoc with it.

Mr. Marsden arrived in the evening, and early the following morning, the whole party—consisting of himself and his two daughters and Mrs. Dinsmore and her six children with their nurses—set out for his home in Kentucky.

They departed without seeing Mildred, who had been so much in the sickroom that they were afraid of her, but left good-byes for her with Mr. Dinsmore.

He made no effort to detain his family but simply remarked to his wife, on taking leave of her, that when she felt it safe to return, he would be happy to see her and their children.

The house seemed strangely quiet and deserted as he turned back into it after seeing them off.

He went up to the sickroom. Mildred was there, moving softly about, supplementing the work of the housemaid with a few skillful touches here and there that seemed to brighten the place wonderfully.

He had said to her at the first, "Mildred, you are not to bear any part of this burden. Mrs. Brown and Aunt Delia are both excellent nurses and will not neglect anything that can be done for her relief or restoration. I cannot have you wearing yourself out."

He said substantially the same thing now, speaking in an undertone that would not disturb the patient, who was sleeping under the influence of medicine.

"I shall not wear myself out, uncle, never fear," she answered in the same low key, smiling up affectionately into his face. "But I cannot be content to stay away all the time, for she seems to cling to me."

"Yes," said Mrs. Brown, coming in. "Miss Mildred has a wonderfully soothing way with her that quiets her in her fits of restlessness and distress, when nothing else can.

"And I think, Mr. Dinsmore," she added in a still lower tone, "that it won't be long that the poor creature will be troubling any of us. I see death in her pale, sunken face now."

Mildred stole into the hall, and her uncle followed her and found her wiping away fast-falling tears.

"Oh, uncle," she sobbed, "what do you think I have discovered? She has been wearing herself out, sitting up half the night for months past, writing articles and stories for newspapers and magazines in order to earn a little more for the support of that mother and sister."

"Indeed!" he said, looking much concerned. "I am very sorry. I would rather have added a hundred dollars to her salary, if I had known it. But unfortunately, it is too late now."

"I can't help feeling angry at them!" cried Mildred. "Why didn't they bear their own burdens, according to the Biblical command? And that brother—and husband! Oh, it is too bad!"

"Have you learned any more of her sad story?" he asked.

"No, sir. She hardly speaks at all except that I have heard her murmur to herself in such a heart-broken way, 'My darling, my darling, oh my darling.' And two or three times she has whispered to me, 'Tell me about Him—that Friend.'"

"That Friend? Whom does she mean?"

"The Lord Jesus—I told her of Him once when I found her sad and troubled, and it seemed to do her some good."

"You are a blessed little comforter! You must have taken lessons from your mother," he said in a moved tone as he turned and went away.

Going downstairs, he ordered his carriage and drove over to Ion.

When he returned, Mrs. Travilla was with him.

It was a glad surprise to Mildred, who knew that Mrs. Travilla would be a greater comfort than anything else save the arrival of her own mother, for here was one with a heart ever tenderly alive to human woe and far more capable than herself of pointing the sufferer to the only true source of help and consolation.

Together they watched, day after day, by the sick and dying bed—for the poor woman had indeed received her death blow in that last and terrible announcement.

She said little, made no complaint, but lay there growing weaker, often lifting her eyes to their faces with a look of hopeless anguish in them that wrung their hearts.

Then Mrs. Travilla would lean over her and in low, tender tones tell of the love and sympathy of Jesus, repeating now one, now another of the many exceeding great and precious promises of His word.

"'As one whom his mother comforteth, so will I comfort you; and ye shall be comforted.'

"'Come unto me, all ye that labor and are heavy laden, and I will give you rest.'

"'I have loved them with an everlasting love.'

"'I will never leave thee nor forsake thee.'

"Ah, if He loves me, why does He send such fearful trials?" she asked one day.

"My dear," said Mrs. Travilla, "He told His disciples, 'In the world ye shall have tribulation; but be of good cheer, I have overcome the world.'

"'We must through such tribulation enter into the kingdom of God.' But 'our light affliction, which is but for a moment, worketh for us a far more exceeding and eternal weight of glory.'

"Trust Him, and He will do for you just what is best. He will give you strength to bear all that He sends, and then He will take you at last to Himself to be unspeakably happy forever and forever."

"I will. I do," she said. "Ah, Miss Keith," turning her sad eyes upon Mildred, who sat near with tears streaming down her cheeks, "I thank God that you were sent here to tell me of this heavenly Friend! For His love is all that sustains me in this dreadful hour."

She closed her eyes, and for some moments they thought she slept. But opening them again, she whispered, "I am dying, but I am not afraid, for He is with me. Ah, how much easier than *his* death—*my darling's!*" she added with a shudder. "Only ten minutes to prepare, and I—I fear he had never found this Friend."

The keenest look of anguish they had ever seen came into her eyes with those words, and for some minutes she was too much overcome to proceed.

When at last she did, it was in tones so low and tremulous that they strained their ears to catch the slight sounds.

"Six years ago we married—secretly—against my parents' wishes. They were right. He was wild—loved wine, cards, fast horses, but me, too! Oh, how I loved him! He was Harry's ruin, too. Both had to fly, and I have never taken his name openly. No one knew what he was to me but my own family. I thought no one need know. Perhaps that was wrong, but how could I bare my heart to a stranger?"

"You were not called upon to do so," Mrs. Travilla said with great emotion, for the sad story had deeply touched her heart.

The mournful eyes turned upon her with a grateful look, then closed in the sleep of utter exhaustion. She passed away that night very calmly and peacefully, trusting in her Redeemer. As Mildred gazed upon the solemn scene, she thanked God that she had been permitted to lead one soul to Him, to smooth one dying pillow, and that Heaven would make amends to the sorely tried one for all she had been called to endure on earth.

Chapter Nineteenth

A lovely being, scarcely formed or molded,
A rose with all its sweetest leaves yet unfolded.

— Byron

ON THE VERANDA of a lordly mansion overlooking a velvety lawn of emerald green spangled with flowers and dotted here and there with giant oaks, magnolias, and orange trees, between which might be caught the silvery gleam of the bright waters of a lakelet beyond, a young child, a lovely little girl of four, was sporting with her nurse, tossing to and fro a many-colored ball with many a sweet baby laugh and shout.

Presently it flew over the railing and rolled away among the flowers in the grass.

"Let's go get it, mammy," said the little one, hurrying down the steps. "Let's toss it on the lawn."

"Wait, honey," returned the nurse, following her. "Ki! Let ole mammy hol' you up to see what's comin' down dar on de wattah."

"Oh, the boat, the boat!" shouted the child, as Aunt Chloe lifted her to her shoulder. "Will it stop, mammy? Is uncle coming on it?

"Dunno, darling; 'spect he is, Aunt Chloe answered, moving on across the lawn in the direction of the little pier where the boat was already rounding to. "Ki! Yes, dar he am, standin' on de deck."

The child clapped her pretty hands with a cry of delight. "I see him! I see him! Please go on, mammy. Now let me down. I want to run to meet him."

A man was stepping ashore, gentlemanly in dress and appearance, of medium height and rather stoutly build, sandy hair and whiskers plentifully sprinkled with gray, and a grave and thoughtful face with a stern mouth but kindly gray eyes.

At the sight of the small, sprightly figure bounding toward him, he set down a valise he carried, stooped and held out his arms, the stern lips relaxing into a smile and the gray eyes twinkling.

In an instant, she was clinging about his neck, the rosebud mouth pressing sweet kisses on his lips.

"Well, my bonny bairn, are you glad to see your old uncle come home?" he asked, holding her for a moment. Then, setting her on her feet and taking her hand, he walked on toward the house, Aunt Chloe and a servant boy with the valise following.

A pleasant-faced matron in a neat muslin dress and cap met them on the veranda.

"Welcome home, sir, Mr. Cameron," she said, shaking hands with him. "Your room's a' ready, and tea will be on the table in ten minutes. Elsie, my bonnie pet, will ye no stay wi' me while uncle changes his linen?"

"Yes, Mrs. Murray, wis you and mammy," the child answered with cheerful acquiescence. "Uncle won't go 'way tomorrow or the nex' day, 'cause he said so."

The child's meals were usually taken alone in the nursery and at earlier hours than those preferred by the older people, which better suited her tender years. But tonight she took tea with her guardian and Mr. Murray, Mrs. Murray sitting opposite him and presiding over the tea urn. Elsie sat between them at his right hand, while Chloe stood at the back of her chair ready to give instant attention to every want and wish.

The evenings were cool enough to make an open wood fire very agreeable, and a fine one blazed and crackled on the hearth in the library, where Mr. Cameron bent his steps on leaving the table.

He had scarcely taken possession of an easy chair beside it when Elsie crept to his side and claimed a seat on his knee.

"Poor bit of a fatherless bairn!" he muttered, as he took her up. "Some folks are, as the good book says, 'without natural affection.'"

"Why, uncle, I's dot a papa, hasn't I?" she asked, catching in an understanding way only the first half of his remark. "Mrs. Murray tells me 'bout him sometimes."

"Yes, so you have," he said, "but he isn't here to take care of his little lassie, you know."

"I wis' he was! I wis' he'd come dus' now!

"And my mamma is in heaven where Jesus is," she prattled on. "My sweet, pretty mamma." Pulling a gold chain about her neck, she drew out from her evening gown a miniature set in gold and diamonds that held a likeness of a very beautiful young girl.

"Dear mamma, sweet, pretty mamma!" she repeated, fondly kissing the pictured face.

"Let me look at it, Elsie," he said, as she was about to return it to its hiding place.

"The bonniest face I ever saw," he mused half aloud, gazing intently upon it. "Woe's me that the sods of the valley should ha' covered it from sight sae soon! Was I wrong? Eh, how could I know that she cared so much for that wild youth? I thought it was the gold he was after, and I think so still."

But he heaved a profound remorseful sigh as he relinquished the miniature to its rightful owner.

As he did so, he caught sight of Aunt Chloe, who was standing near, her dark eyes fixed on him with an expression of the keenest sorrow mingled with some reproach.

"She blames me," he thought uneasily. "Well, well, I meant it all for the best."

"Aunt Chloe," he said, speaking aloud, "bring me the parcel you'll find on my dressing table.

She left the room and presently returned, bringing what he had sent her for.

"Something for you, Elsie," he said, laying it in her lap.

It was loosely wrapped in brown paper that she quickly unfolded with her small fingers, bringing to light a large, beautiful, and handsomely dressed doll.

"Oh, oh! See, mammy, see!" she cried in delight. "Such a big dolly! Biggest of all I's dot."

Then she thanked the giver with kisses and smiles and sweet words of baby gratitude, for she was a child of most a grateful and loving disposition.

Mrs. Murray must be called in to see and admire the new treasure. Then with it hugged closely in her arms, the delighted darling bade goodnight and suffered her mammy to lead her away to bed.

"What a bonny wee 'un she is! One canna think well o' the father that neglects her," remarked Mr. Cameron, as the tiny, fairy-like figure disappeared through the doorway.

"It's unaccountable, and the whiles makes me hae grave doubts of the reality of his love for the mother," said the housekeeper. "But if once he got sight o' the bairn, it would surely be different. Who could see the bit winsome thing and not love her dearly? Can ye no manage to get him here by hook or by crook, Mr. Cameron?"

"I cannot say that I'm over anxious," he answered dryly. "He's too fiery and hotheaded a youth to deal comfortably with. Besides, he's away in Europe."

"Ah! When will he return?"

"Indeed, Mrs. Murray, I got no hint o' that, except that his stay was likely to be lengthy."

She had brought in her accounts of household expenditures for the past month, and some time was spent in going over them and conversing on various business matters.

"Mr. Cameron," she said, as the interview was about to close, "life and health are both uncertain wi' us all. In case anything should happen to you, sir, what—"

"I will give you the address of my solicitor and o' the bairn's grandfather," he said, without waiting for the conclusion of her sentence. Turning to his writing desk, he wrote both on a card, which he handed to her, saying, "It would be advisable for you or the overseer to send them both word immediately if aught occur to deprive me of the ability to attend to the affairs o' the estate and the welfare o' the bit lassie."

Scarcely a week had elapsed when Mrs. Murray found reason to be thankful for this act of prudent foresight. Mr. Cameron was taken suddenly and violently ill, soon became delirious, and after a few days of suffering, breathed his last without an interval in which he could have attended to business, however important.

As soon as it was known that the illness was likely to terminate fatally, letters were dispatched to the addresses given.

The lawyer, living no further away than New Orleans, was able to reach Viamede in time for the funeral. But it would take weeks for the letter to Mr. Dinsmore to wend its way to Roselands.

Little Elsie saw nothing of her guardian after he was taken sick. She was not shown the corpse, and during the funeral, her nurse had her away in a distant part of the grounds.

"She's too young to be saddened wi' thoughts o' death and the grave," said Mrs. Murray. "We'll just tell her, when she asks for her uncle, that he's gone to the beautiful heaven where the Savior is—and her sweet, pretty mamma, too. And she'll hae only pleasant thoughts about it, the darling pet!"

The good woman had a very strong, motherly affection for the lovely little one and was more concerned in regard to the possible, not to say probable, separation from her consequent upon Mr. Cameron's death than with any other question touching her own earthly future. She did not know what disposal would be made of the child, but she was resolved not to endure separation if it could be avoided, even by a considerable monetary sacrifice.

The lawyer could tell her nothing except that the child's father would now assume entire control of both her person and property.

"Then," she said with the tears stealing down her cheeks, "I fear we may have to part. But I will ever comfort myself with the thought that God reigns and that mon's heart is in His hand as the rivers of waters, so that He can turn it whithersoever He will."

"You seem strongly attached to her," remarked the lawyer. "Well, she's a pretty little creature and a great heiress. The estate was large at the time of her grandfather's death, and it has flourished under my friend Cameron's care. His investments were always judicious. In fact, he couldn't have handled the funds more wisely and carefully if it had been his own. Mr. Dinsmore has been sent for, you say?"

"The grandfather, sir. The father's far away in Europe, sir."

"Ah! Rather unfortunate, I do fear. Well, Mrs. Murray, I have finished the business that brought me here, and I shall leave by the next boat, which passes, I understand, half an hour from this," he concluded, consulting his watch.

"Yes," she said, "but you will first step into the

dining room and take some refreshment, will you not, sir? It is quite ready."

He accepted the invitation, and while sipping his teas, said, "I shall see Mr. Dinsmore in New Orleans. He will doubtless call upon me there before coming on to Viamede, and you may depend, Mrs. Murray, that if I have any influence, it will be exerted in favor of the plan of leaving the little girl in your care."

"I thank you, sir," she said. "I love the sweet bairn as I loved my own, now all gone before to the heavenly rest, and perhaps, as they hae never seemed to care to trouble wi' her, they may be willing to continue her in my charge."

Mrs. Murray was by no means the only one at Viamede who dreaded the changes that might come as an indirect consequence of the death of Elsie's guardian. There were many anxious hearts among the older and more informed of the servants. Would the little mistress, whom they fairly idolized, be carried away from them? Would there be a change of overseers? Would any of them be taken away from their kindred and the plantation that was their home?

Work had been suspended on account of the funeral. It was over, and returning to their accustomed haunts about the mansion and the quarter, they collected in little groups here and there, looking sadly into each other's faces and talking in subdued tones with many a dubious shake of the head and not a few tears dropped to the memory of the fair young creature who had left them after four years to lie down beside her parents in the family burial ground on a grassy slope not far away.

Ah, could they but have kept her! She was so sweet, so gentle, so kind.

Presently, Aunt Chloe and her young charge, taking the quarter on their way to the mansion, appeared among them, the baby girl looking wondrously like her whom they mourned, with the same fair, oval face, large, lustrous, hazel eyes, golden brown hair, and sunny smile.

They gathered about her with honeyed words of endearments, kissing the small white hands, the golden ringlets, even the hem of her richly embroidered white dress. She scattered gracious and winsome words and smiles like a little queen among her loyal subjects.

It was truly the homage of the heart, for scarcely one of them would have hesitated to risk life and limb in her service.

She dispensed her favors with great impartiality and was borne to the house on the shoulders of several of these ardent admirers, each taking his turn in carrying her part of the way that all might share in the privilege, since the loving little heart would not favor one to the rejection of the others.

It was just as Mr. Coonly, the solicitor, was about to take his departure that the baby girl was thus borne in triumph to the veranda and set down there all flushed and rosy and crowing with delight.

"Nice ride, Uncle Ben, and all you other uncles," she said, kissing her hand to them. "Mammy will get you some cakes."

"She's a beautiful child!" exclaimed the solicitor in an aside to Mrs. Murray.

"Yes, sir, and a dear bairn, as sweet and as good as she is fair."

"Will you give me a good-bye kiss, my little dear?" he asked, stepping toward her.

"Yes," she said, holding up her rosebud mouth. "But I don't know you. Did you come to see uncle? Where is he?"

He gave her a puzzled look, then saying, "I haven't time to tell you now, my little girl," hurried away.

She looked after him a moment, then turning to Mrs. Murray, repeated her question.

"Gone away, darling," was the answer. "Now come in and eat your supper, and then we'll have a nice bit o' talk."

CHAPTER TWENTIETH

Not mine—yet dear to me—fair, fragrant blossom
Of a fair tree—
Crushed to the earth in life's first glorious summer—
Thou'rt dear to me,
Child of the lost, the buried, and the sainted.

—MRS. WELBY

THE HOUSEKEEPER'S ROOM, to which she now led the little Elsie, was a cheery, pleasant place. On a small, round table covered with snowy satin-like damask and a service of glittering silverware, cut glass, and Sevres china, a tempting little repast was laid out for the two.

Mrs. Murray took her seat, and Aunt Chloe lifted Elsie into a high chair opposite.

The little one closed her eyes, folded her baby hands, and bent reverently over her plate while Mrs. Murray asked in a few simple words a blessing on their food.

Aunt Chloe waited on them while they ate, devoting herself particularly to her infant charge, as another servant was also in attendance, then withdrew to the servants' hall to eat her own supper.

And now, Mrs. Murray, seating herself in a low rocking chair, took the child on her lap.

Elsie nestled in her arms, laid her head on her shoulder, and softly patting her cheek, said, "I love you, Mrs. Murray."

"I dinna doubt it, my sweet, bit lassie, and I love you, too—dearly, dearly," the good woman returned, accompanying the words with tender, motherly caresses. "And the dear Lord Jesus loves you better still, darling. Never forget that. Never doubt that you are His own precious lambkin and that He is always near to hear you when you pray."

"Yes, I know," answered the child. "Jesus loves little children. Jesus loves little Elsie. And someday He'll let Elsie go to live wis Him and wis her sweet, pretty mamma. Jesus loves my mamma and lets her live 'long wis Him."

"Yes, dear, she is there in that happy land. And uncle has gone to be with her now."

The child started, lifted her head, and gazing earnestly and questioningly into the housekeeper's eyes, asked, "Uncle gone, too? Will he come back again?"

"No, dear bairn. They never want to come back from that blessed land, for they are so happy there with the dear Savior."

"Why didn't he take Elsie 'long?" cried the child, bursting into tears. "I want to go dere, too."

"Jesus didn't send for you this time, sweet pet," the housekeeper answered with emotion, folding the little form closer to her heart. "He would have you and me bide here yet a bit, but someday He will call us home, too. He's getting a very lovely home ready for us there."

"For my papa, too?"

"I trust so, darling."

"Where is my papa? Why doesn't he come to Elsie?

"I don't know, my bonnie bairn. I think he will come someday."

"And take Elsie on his knee, and kiss her, and love her?"

"Surely, surely, darling. And you have a grandpa, who will be here before many days pass, I trust."

"Grandpa that's gone to heaven?"

"No, that is Grandpa Grayson, your sweet mamma's father. This is Grandpa Dinsmore, your papa's father."

The child looked thoughtful for a moment. Then with a joyous smile, she exclaimed, "Elsie's so glad! I wish he'd come now. Elsie will love him ever so much."

"May the Lord open his heart to love you in return, sweet bairnie," sighed the good woman. "But not to take you frae me," she added mentally.

The child pleaded for "stories 'bout mamma, 'bout Elsie's mamma when she was a little girlie and played wis her little brothers and sisters."

Mrs. Murray, having been housekeeper at Viamede for nearly twenty years, had a plentiful store of these laid up in her memory. Each one had been repeated for the little girl's entertainment a score of times or more, but repetition seemed to have no power to lessen their interest for her.

"Why doesn't Elsie have brothers and sisters?" she asked, during a pause in the narration. "Elsie do want some so bad!"

"Our Father didna see fit to give you any, dear bairn. So, you must try to be content without," Mrs. Murray answered with a tender caress. "We canna have all we would like in this world, but when we get home where the dear Lord Jesus is, we'll have nothing left to wish for. Our cup o' joy will be full to overflowing. Now bid me goodnight, my wee bonnie, bonnie darling, for here's mammy come to take you to bed."

The child complied with alacrity. She and her mammy were devotedly attached to each other and had seldom been apart for an hour since the little girl first saw the light.

And the nurse, though uneducated, was as simple-hearted and earnest a Christian as Mrs. Murray herself. She faithfully carried out the dying injunction of her young mother, to try to teach her little one, from her earliest years, to love and fear the Lord.

She talked and sang to her of Jesus before she was a year old, and as soon as she began to speak, she taught her to kneel night and morning with folded hands and lisp her little prayers.

She also told her sweet stories of the mother she had never known, of the beautiful home where she had gone, of the loving Savior who was with her there and was also on earth watching over her darling.

Every night she rocked her to sleep in her arms, soothing her to rest with these ever new stories and sweet melodies.

Aunt Chloe had known sorrows many and bitter,

not the least of them the untimely death of Elsie's mother. With none left to her in whose veins her own blood flowed, she clung to this nursling with a love that would have hesitated at no sacrifice for the good of its object and with a passionate, yearning tenderness that would have led her to choose death for herself rather than separation. The big tears chased each other down her cheeks at the bare thought of such a possibility, as she held her sleeping treasure in her arms that night.

She knew little of the child's father and nothing whatever of the grandfather or any other of the paternal relatives, and her heart warned there might be trouble in store for herself and her beloved charge.

Someone came in softly through the open door, and Chloe looked up with tears still on her cheeks to find the housekeeper close at her side. "What is it, Aunt Chloe?" she asked in a tone of alarm. "The dear bairn is not ill?"

Chloe only shook her head, while her bosom heaved with half-suppressed sobs.

"Ah, I know what it is!" sighed Mrs. Murray. "Your heart trembles wi' the vera same fear that oppresses mine—lest the darling o' our dear love be torn frae our arms. But we winna greet for sorrow that may never come. We winna doubt His love and power, Him Who doeth all things well. Let us no forget that He loves her better by far than we do.

"Said the saintly Rutherford, 'I shall charge my soul to believe and to wait for Him, and shall follow His providence, and not go before it, nor stay behind it.' Let us make the same resolve, Aunt Chloe, and be

happy while we may, be happy always, for His loving kindness shall never fail.

"Mind His word, 'I am the Lord who exercise
loving kindness, judgment, and righteousness in the
earth, for in these things I delight, saith the Lord.'"

"Ef dey take my bressed lamb away, dis ole heart
break for sure!" sobbed Chloe, clasping the child
closer. "I'se done gone los' eberyting else!"

"No, no, Aunt Chloe! Not the Lord!"

"No, missus, not de Lord! Dat true. Hope He
forgib de sinful word!"

"And not the hope of heaven!"

"No, no missus, not dat either, bress His holy
name!"

"It is a world of trial, Aunt Chloe, but He never
sends one that is na needful for us, and 'when His
people cannot have a providence of silk and roses,
they must be content with such a one as He carveth
out for them.' 'How soon would grace freeze without
a cross!'"

"Dat true, missus, an' we mus' take de cross first or
we can't hab de crown at de las'," she assented with
a heavy sigh. "Missus, do you know what gwine be
done now? Will dey sell de plantation?"

"Oh, no! It belongs to the bairn."

"De servants?"

"I don't think there is any danger there, either."

Aunt Chloe breathed more freely. "Will Massa
Dinsmore come an' lib heyah hisself?" she asked.

"That I canna tell," Mrs. Murray said, shaking her
head and sighing slightly. "But, Aunt Chloe, I dinna
think ye need fear bein' parted frae the bairn. They

may take her frae me, but they'll no be likely to separate her from her mammy; wherever she goes you will, in a' probability, go also."

Chloe asked if Elsie was to be taken away from Viamede, to which the housekeeper answered that she did not know. Indeed, nothing could be known till Mr. Dinsmore came.

"But," she added, "whether the sweet bairn's home be here or elsewhere, an attendant will be needed, and I see no reason why the old mammy, who loves her sae dearly, should be exchanged for another. I wad be blithe to think myself as secure o' bein' kept near her, but they're no sae likely to want a housekeeper as a nurse, should they decide to change her abode."

"Tank de Lord for dat!" exclaimed Aunt Chloe, half under her breath, as she rose and gently laid the sleeping child in her bed. "I tink my bressed lamb neber be happy widout her ole mammy to lub her, an' I hopes dey'll let you stay, too, missus. I's afraid Massa Dinsmore not care much 'bout his little chile. 'Cause ef he do, why he neber come for to see her?"

The words sounded to Mrs. Murray like the echo of her own thoughts.

"I dinna understand it," she whispered, bending over the little one to press a tender kiss on the softly rounded, rosy cheek. "I canna comprehend it, but the sweet wee 'un has had a happy life thus far. And please God, Aunt Chloe, she'll ne'er want for love while He leaves her in our care."

Chapter Twenty-First

A sweet, heartlifting cheerfulness,
Like springtime of the year,
Seemed ever on her steps to wait.

—Mrs. Hale

"I SHOULD LIKE to have a little chat with you, Milly, my dear," Mr. Dinsmore said pleasantly, looking across the table at her where she sat behind the tea urn—her accustomed place now in Mrs. Dinsmore's absence. "Can you give me an hour or two of your company in the library this evening?"

"Just as much of it as you may happen to want, uncle," she answered brightly.

"Thank you," he said. "I rejoice every day in having you here. It would be extremely dull without you, but I wonder sometimes how you keep up your spirits. Nearly six weeks since Mrs. Dinsmore went away, and nobody in the house the greater part of the time but yourself, the housekeeper, and servants."

"It is a little lonely sometimes," she acknowledged, "but I have you at meals and in the evening, generally, now and then a call from one of the neighbors, and almost every day I ride over to Ion and spend an hour or two with dear Mrs. Travilla. So, with the assis-

tance of books, music, drawing, and writing letters to
mother and the rest, I find the days pass quite rapidly."

"Ah! There is a great deal in being disposed to be
contented!" he said smiling. "You are like your
mother in that, too.

"We have not yet succeeded in finding a suitable
person to fill Miss Worth's place, and that is one reason your aunt gives for lingering so long at her sister's.
The place affords excellent educational advantages."

There was a little more desultory chat, and then,
having finished their meal, they repaired to the
library. Mildred was more than a little curious to
learn what her uncle had to say, for she felt quite
certain from his manner that it was something of
unusual importance.

He drew an easy chair to the fire, seated her
comfortably therein, then turning away, he paced the
floor for some moments in silence and with an
abstracted air and clouded brow.

She watched him furtively, wondering more and
more at his evident disturbance.

At last, heaving a profound sigh, he seated himself
near her.

"You are already acquainted, Mildred, so your
Aunt Wealthy informed me," he began in the tone of
one who approaches a very distasteful subject, "with
a certain chapter in my son Horace's history, which
I would be exceedingly glad to bury in forgetfulness.
But circumstances have now rendered that impossible, since the child of that most imprudent, ill-
advised marriage has seen fit to live, and of course
her existence cannot be entirely ignored."

Mildred was growing rather indignant. Her color heightened, and her eyes sparkled, though it was all unperceived by him, as his face was half averted.

"Is there anything wrong with her, uncle?" she ventured, as he came to a pause.

"Wrong with her?" he echoed. "Heaven forbid! It is bad enough as it is. But, indeed, I have never taken the trouble to ask. In fact, I believe I unconsciously hoped she might never cross my path. But," and again he sighed, "that is past. A letter I received this morning from Louisiana brings news of the death of her guardian—that is, you understand, the man who was left guardian to her mother and the property—which, by the way, is very large."

Mildred began to listen with eager interest. She had wished very much to see Horace's child. Could it be that her wish was to be gratified?

"The child is heir to it all," Mr. Dinsmore went on. "The mother married and died under age, and by the conditions of the will, the property remained in Mr. Cameron's care—the child also, Horace not caring to remove her. Now, however, the responsibility all falls upon me in his absence. I must now look after both estate and heiress. It involves an immediate journey to Louisiana and probably a stay of some weeks to get matters settled.

"I must bring the child home with me, as of course leaving her there with only servants is not to be thought of, and, in fact, I know of no other home for her, for being a mere babe, she cannot be sent to a boarding school.

"I anticipate some complaint from Mrs. Dinsmore.

She will not like it, I know, but it really cannot be helped and need not add to her cares in the least."

"Poor, little, motherless thing!" sighed Mildred softly, and as Mr. Dinsmore gave her a hasty glance, he saw that her eyes were full of tears.

"It is a pity about her," he said. "Strange that she was destined to survive her mother. It would really have been so much more comfortable for all parties if she had not."

"It does seem as though it might have been a happy thing for her," Mildred answered dryly.

But he did not notice the tone. Turning to her with a smile, "How would you like to go with me to Louisiana?" he asked.

Her face grew radiant with delight at the bare suggestion. "Oh, uncle, how delightful! But it would be a very expensive journey, wouldn't it?" she asked, and her countenance fell.

"That would be my concern, since I invite you," he said, laughing and playfully tapping her cheek. "Where did you learn to be so very careful and economical? Don't trouble yourself about expense. I shall consider the pleasure of your company cheaply purchased at the cost of settling all the bills. Now will you go?"

"Yes, indeed, and thank you a thousand times! If—"

"If, what? Father and mother give their consent? There's no time to ask it, as I leave the day after tomorrow, but I am sure it would not be withheld. So we'll do as we please first and ask for their permission afterward."

"Yes," Mildred responded after only a moment's musing, "I feel convinced that they would be very glad to have me accept your generous offer. It is such an opportunity as I am not likely to meet again."

The remainder of the evening was devoted to the writing of a long, bright, and cheery letter to her mother, telling of the pleasant prospect before her and promising that the home circle should share in the enjoyments of her trip so far as descriptions of scenery and adventures, written in her best style, could enable them to do.

Mildred's letters had come to be considered a very great treat in that little community, their reception looked forward to with eager anticipation. The enjoyment would be doubled when they told of the scenes new and fascinating and of Cousin Horace's little girl, in whom they already felt so deep an interest.

Mildred had enjoyed her visit to Roselands, but since the death of Miss Worth, the atmosphere of the house had seemed somewhat lonely and depressing. So she was very glad of her uncle's invitation, which promised a change in every way delightful.

The journey was tedious and wearisome in those days, compared to what it would be now: staging across the country to the nearest point on the Mississippi, thence by steamboat to New Orleans — where they remained several weeks while Mr. Dinsmore was engaged in making arrangements in regard to the portion of little Elsie's inheritance that lay in the Crescent City — then on to Viamede.

It pleased Mildred that this part of their trip was to be all the way by water. After they entered Teche

Bayou, it seemed to her like a passage through fairy land, so bright were the skies, so balmy the breezes, so rich and varied was the scenery—swamps, forest, plain, gliding by in rapid succession. Her eyes roved over the richest vegetation, resting now upon some cool, shady dell gaily carpeted with flowers, now on a lawn covered with velvet-like grass of emerald green and nobly shaded by magnificent oaks and magnolias, now catching sight of a lordly villa peeping through its groves of orange trees, and later of a tall, white sugar house or a long row of cabins, the homes of the laborers.

It was a new region of country to Mr. Dinsmore as well as herself, and he remarked that he considered the sight of it a sufficient recompense in itself for the trouble and expense of the journey.

"But besides that," he added, "I have had the satisfaction of learning that the estate is even much larger than I supposed. That Scotsman was faithful to his trust and very shrewd, too, in making investments, and his death gives Horace control, during the child's minority, of a princely income."

"Then you do not regret his marriage so much as you did?" Mildred said inquiringly.

"I did not say that," was the cold, almost stern reply, and she said no more.

CHAPTER
TWENTY-SECOND

I would that thou might'st ever be
As beautiful as now;
That time might ever leave as free
Thy yet unwritten brow.

—WILLIS

"WHEN WILL MY drampa come?" little Elsie asked again and again, and finding that no one could tell her, she set herself to watch the passing boats, often coaxing her mammy out upon the lawn or down to the very water's edge in her eagerness for a sight of him and her very first look into the face of a relative.

She was fond of Mrs. Murray, as she had been of Mr. Cameron, and clung with ardent affection to her mammy. Yet the baby heart yearned for parental love, and naturally she expected to receive it from her grandfather.

Had she heard that her father was coming, she would have been wild with joy, and so, the arrival of her grandfather seemed the next best thing that could happen.

Mildred knew nothing of the child's anticipations, yet her heart ached for the little creature as she perceived how determined Mr. Dinsmore was to shut her out of his.

"She's a fortunate little miss," he remarked of her as they came in sight of a sugar and orange plantation exceeding in size and fertility almost any they had passed. The captain of the boat, pointing it out, said, "That's Viamede—the old Grayson place."

They were sweeping by a large sugar house, then came to an immense orange orchard, and then a long and wide stretch of lawn with the loveliest carpet of velvety green and most magnificent shade trees they had ever beheld. With their great arms and abundant foliage, they half concealed a lordly mansion set far back among them.

So surpassingly lovely was the whole scene that for a moment Mildred could have echoed her uncle's words and almost found it in her heart to envy the young heiress of it all. But the next moment, she said to herself, "No, no, not for all this would I be so lonely and loveless as she is, the poor, little, forlorn girl!"

The boat rounded to at the little pier. Close by, in the shade of a great oak, stood an elderly woman with a child in her arms—a little girl of fairy-like form and face perfect in outline and feature. Her complexion was of a dazzling brilliance, her countenance radiant with delight, as she watched the travelers stepping ashore.

"This is she, I presume," Mr. Dinsmore said coolly, halting in front of the two. "What's your name, child?"

"Elsie Dinsmore," she answered, her lip quivering and the large, soft eyes filling with tears. "I fot it was my drampa comin'."

"And so it is," he said, slightly touched by her evident disappointment. "Have you a kiss for me?"

For answer, she threw both arms about his neck, as he bent toward her, and pressed her red lips to his.

He disengaged himself rather hastily, stepping back to give place to Mildred, who, gazing with delight upon the beautiful little creature, was eagerly awaiting her turn.

"You darling!" she cried, clasping the child in a warm embrace. "This is Cousin Milly, and she is going to love you dearly, dearly!"

"Thank you, Miss," said Aunt Chloe with tears in her eyes. "And welcome to Viamede, Miss. Welcome, Massa," she said, dropping a curtsy to each.

Mrs. Murray and several servants now came hurrying toward them. There were more curtsies and welcomes, and the baggage was seized and quickly transported to the house, while the travelers, Mrs. Murray, and Aunt Chloe with her little charge, followed it leisurely.

Mildred was filled with delight at the beauty surrounding her, yet she was more attracted by the child than by all else. She turned toward her with an affectionate smile, and the little one, now walking by her nurse's side, returned it with one of rare sweetness. She ran to her and slipped a tiny, soft hand into hers.

"Is she not beautiful, uncle?" Mildred asked with enthusiasm, at the first opportunity for doing so without being overheard.

"She's no Dinsmore," he said coldly. "There's not a trace of Horace's looks about her. She must be all Grayson, I presume."

"Oh, how can he!" thought Mildred. "How can he harden his heart so against anything so gentle and beautiful?"

They were standing on the veranda for a moment, admiring the view and watching the departure of the boat that had brought them, while Mrs. Murray was busy giving directions in regard to the disposal of their luggage.

A suite of delightful apartments had been appropriated for Mildred's use during her stay. Conducted there by Aunt Chloe and her nursling, she took possession with great content . With the assistance of a skillful waiting maid, also placed at her service, she soon arrayed her neat figure in a becoming dinner dress, little Elsie and her mammy looking on admiringly all the while.

"Isn't my cousin *so* pretty, mammy?" whispered the little one.

Mildred heard, and turning with a pleased smile, she held out her hand to the child. "Won't you come and sit on cousin's lap a little while? I can tell you about your dear papa, for I know him."

The child's face grew radiant, and she hastened to accept the invitation.

"Oh," she said, "please do! Will he come here soon? I want to see my papa! I want to kiss him and love him."

The soft eyes filled with sad tears, and the red lips quivered.

Mildred clasped the little form close in her arms and kissed the sweet, fair face over and over, exclaiming in tremulous tones," You dear, precious baby! If he could only see you, I'm sure he couldn't help loving you with all his heart!"

The travelers were summoned to the dinner table, and little Elsie partook with them, conducting herself with the utmost propriety.

"She seems a well-behaved child," her grandfather remarked graciously. "How old are you, my dear? Can you tell?"

"I's four," piped the bird-like voice. "I's a big girl now, drampa. I'm too big to be naughty, but sometimes I's not very good."

"Ah! that's honest," he said with a rather amused smile. "Well, what do they do to you when you are naughty?"

"When I was a little girl, mammy put me in de corner sometimes."

"And what now that you are so large?"

"She jus' say, 'Jesus not pleased wis my darlin' child when she naughty.'"

"You don't mind that, do you?" he asked curiously.

She looked at him with innocent, wondering eyes. "Elsie loves Jesus. Elsie wants Jesus to love her and make her His little lamb. She asks Him to do it every day."

"Stuff!" he muttered in a tone of annoyance, but tears of both joy and thankfulness welled up in Mildred's eyes.

"Blessed baby!" she thought. "You will not have a lonely, loveless life if you have so soon begun to seek the dear Savior. Ah, how my mother's heart will rejoice to hear this!"

On coming to the table, the little one had folded her tiny hands, and bending with closed eyes over her plate, murmured a short grace. But Mr. Dinsmore, busying himself with carving a fowl, did not seem to notice it, yet it had not escaped him. He was watching the child furtively and with far more interest than he would have liked to admit.

"I'm afraid they're making a canting hypocrite of her," he said to Mildred when they had retired to the drawing room.

"Oh, uncle, do not say that!" exclaimed Mildred. "It is just the way my dear mother, whom you admire so much, trains and teaches her children."

"Ah!" he said. "Then I shall have to retract."

"What pretty manners she has, uncle, both at the table and elsewhere," remarked Mildred. "She handles fork and spoon as deftly as possible, and she is so gentle and refined in all she does and says."

"Yes," he said with some pride, "I trust an uncouth, ill-mannered Dinsmore might be considered an anomaly, indeed."

"Then you acknowledge that she is a Dinsmore?" Mildred said playfully.

"Have I ever denied that she was Horace's child?" he answered with a smile.

"I wish he could see her at this moment. I am sure that he could not help feeling that he had good reason to be proud of her," Mildred said, approaching a window that looked out upon the lawn, where the little one was wandering about gathering flowers. "See, uncle! Is not every movement full of grace?"

"You seem to be quite bewitched with her," he returned good humoredly, following the direction of her glance. "Children's movements are not apt to be ungraceful, I think.

"This is a fine, old mansion," he went on, "and seems to be well-furnished throughout. Have you been in the library? No? Then come, we will visit it now. Your heart will rejoice at the sight of the well-filled bookshelves.

"Ah, I knew it!" he said, watching the expression of keen satisfaction with which she regarded them when he had taken her there.

They consisted largely of very valuable works in every branch of literature, and Mildred's sole regret was that she would have so little time to examine and enjoy them.

There were also some fine paintings and beautiful pieces of statuary in the room, and indeed scattered through all the principal rooms of the house, the drawing room being especially rich in them.

They lingered for some time over these works of art and then went out upon the veranda, presently wandering on from that to the lawn, where they strolled about a little and finally seated themselves under a beautiful magnolia.

"Ah, see what a pretty picture they make!" Mildred exclaimed, glancing in the direction of another, at some little distance, in whose shade Aunt Chloe was seated upon the grass with Elsie in her lap, both busy with the flowers they had been gathering.

"Yes," said Mr. Dinsmore, "and what a striking contrast! The child so young and delicately fair and the nurse so elderly. She seems much attached to her charge."

"Yes, indeed! You would not think of separating them, uncle?"

"Certainly not! Why should I?"

Mildred answered only with a pleased look, for at that moment little Elsie left her mammy and came running with a lovely bouquet in each hand.

"One for you, drampa, and one for Cousin Milly," she said, dropping a graceful little curtsy as she presented them.

"Thank you, dear. How pretty they are!" Mildred said, kissing her.

"Humph! What shall I do with it?" Mr. Dinsmore asked, accepting his.

"Put it in your buttonhole," said the child. "That's the way uncle does."

"Uncle? Who is he? You have none that you ever saw, so far as I know."

"Massa Cameron, sah," explained Aunt Chloe, coming up. "He always tole de chile call him dat."

"Well, she needn't do so any more. I don't like it. Do you hear?" he said to Elsie. "Don't call that man uncle again; he was no relation whatever to you."

His tone spoke displeasure, and the little one drew back to the shelter of her mammy's arms with a frightened look, her lip trembling and her soft, hazel eyes full of tears.

"There, there!" he said, more gently. "Don't cry. I'm not angry with you. You knew no better."

He rose and wandered away toward the rear of the mansion, and Mildred drew Elsie to a seat upon her lap, caressing her tenderly.

"Sweet little girl," she said, "cousin loves you dearly already, and I cannot bear to see tears in those eyes. Tell me about your sweet, pretty mamma."

"Here she is, cousin. Don't you love her, too?" prattled the babe, drawing forth the miniature from her bosom and quickly forgetting her momentary grief in displaying it. "She's gone up to heaven to stay wis Jesus, and some day he'll take Elsie there, too."

"Mildred," said Mr. Dinsmore, coming back, "I hear there are fine saddle horses in the stables. If I order two of them brought around, will you ride over the plantation with me?"

"Gladly!" she said, putting the child gently down and rising with alacrity. "I will go at once and don my riding habit. You shall tell me the rest another time, little pet."

Already enthusiastic admirers of Viamede, they returned from their ride doubly impressed with its beauties.

"It seems an earthly paradise," Mildred wrote to her mother, "and the little owner is the loveliest, most fairy-like creature you can imagine—so sweet, so gentle, so beautiful, and as good as she is pretty. Mrs. Murray tells me she is generosity itself, and she doesn't believe there is a grain of selfishness in her nature. Elsie showed me her mamma's miniature, and she is so sweet and beautiful that I do not wonder that Cousin Horace lost his heart at first sight."

It was not until the next day that this letter was written. Mildred had enough to do that day in looking about her and making acquaintance with Elsie and her attendants.

After tea, Mr. Dinsmore being closeted with the overseer, she made her way to the nursery, coaxed the little one into her lap again, though indeed no great amount of persuasion was needed, and amused her for an hour or two with stories and nursery rhymes.

But the child's bedtime drew near, and with a tender goodnight and a lingering, loving caress, Mildred left her and went down to the drawing room.

Her uncle was not there, and passing out to the veranda, she fell into a chat with Mrs. Murray, whom she found seated there enjoying the beautiful scenery and the soft evening air.

Their talk turned naturally to Viamede and the Grayson family—particularly Horace Dinsmore's wife, the last of the family to bear the name. Mrs. Murray gave many details that were of great interest to her listener.

"She was very lovely," she said, "baith in person and in character. She was a sweet, earnest, child-like Christian, and the bairn is wonderfully like her. She seemed to me a lamb of the fold from her very birth, and nae doot in answer to the mother's prayers. Ye ken, Miss Keith, that she lived scarce a week after her babe was born. All her anxiety was that she should be trained up in the nurture and admonition o' the Lord, her constant prayer that He would be pleased to mak' her His own.

"The bit bairnie isna perfect, of course, but quite as near it as grown folk. It's very evident that she tries to please the blessed Savior. She grieves when she has done wrong, and she canna rest till she's been awi' by hersel' to beg His forgiveness.

"I tell her aboot the new heart God gives His children, and that He will give it to a' such as ask earnestly. She will look up in my face with those great innocent eyes and answer, 'Yes, Mrs. Murray, and I do ask earnestly every day.'"

The old lady brushed away a tear, and her voice was slightly tremulous, as she added, "Mr. Cameron used to fret a bit sometimes that she was too gude to live—like her mother before her, he wad say. But I canna think early piety any sign that life will be short. Except, indeed, that when the work o' grace is fully done, glory follows. She's come o' a God-fearing race, Miss Keith, and the Lord's aye faithful to His promise—showing mercy to thousands o' generations o' them that love Him and keep His commandments.

CHAPTER TWENTY-THIRD

She was like
A dream of poetry, that may not be
Written or told—exceeding beautiful.

—WILLIS

As MILDRED SAT at the open window of her dressing room the next morning, enjoying the beauty of the landscape, the delicious perfume of myriads of dew-laden shrubs and flowers, the gentle summer breeze, and the glad songs of the birds, her ear caught the patter of little feet in the corridor without and a gentle rap upon her door.

She made haste to open the door to the hall, and a bright vision of loveliness met her view—a tiny form arrayed in spotless white of some thin, delicate fabric trimmed with costly lace and a broad sash of pale blue, with slippers to match. She had a shining mass of golden brown curls clustering about the sweet face and rippling over the fair neck and shoulders.

The soft eyes looked up lovingly into her face, and the rosebud mouth was held up for a kiss.

"Good morning, cousin," said the bird-like voice. "Did Elsie 'sturb you coming so soon?"

"No, darling, indeed you don't!" cried Mildred, giving her a rapturous embrace. "I can't see too much of you, dear little pet! Will you come and sit in my lap while we have another nice talk?"

The child hesitated. "Don't you want to come wis me, cousin, and see my mamma when she was a little girl and my mamma's things?"

"I should like it greatly," Mildred answered, suffering herself to be led along the corridor and into an open door at its farther end.

Here, she found herself in a beautiful boudoir. Evidently no expense had been spared in furnishing it in the must luxurious and tasteful manner. Even Mildred's inexperienced eye recognized the costly nature of many of its adornments, though there was nothing gaudy about them.

Elsie led her directly to a full-length, life-sized picture of a little girl of ten or twelve, before which Mildred stood transfixed with delight—face and form were so lifelike and so exquisitely lovely.

She gazed upon it for many minutes with ravished eyes, then glancing at the little one standing by her side, she said half aloud. "Beautiful as it is, I do not believe it is flattered. For it is just what she will be six or eight years hence."

"It's my mamma when she was a little girl," Elsie said. "And this," she added, drawing the miniature from her bosom, "is my mamma when she was a lady."

Mildred gazed upon it again long and earnestly, thinking as before that there was abundant excuse for her cousin Horace's passion and his inconsolable grief over his loss.

There were two other portraits in the room, which Elsie said were Grandpa and Grandma Grayson. She pointed out, too, her mother's writing desk and her worktable. A dainty basket lay upon the last, a little gold thimble and a bit of embroidery with the needle still sticking in it, just as it had been laid down on the morning of the day on which the little one first saw the light.

It was Aunt Chloe, coming in search of her nursling, who told Mildred this.

But Elsie drew her on through a beautiful dressing room into a spacious and elegantly furnished bedroom beyond. Aunt Chloe, following, pointed out with bitter weeping the pillow on which the dying head had lain and described the last hours of her idolized mistress. She told of her mournful leave-taking of her little babe and her dying injunction to her to bring her up to love the Lord Jesus.

It was all intensely interesting and deeply affecting to Mildred.

"Don't cry, mammy, you dear ole mammy!" said Elsie, pulling her nurse down into a chair and, with her own tiny white handkerchief, wiping away her tears. "Don't cry, 'cause dear Mamma is very happy wis Jesus, and you and Elsie are goin' dere, too, someday. An' den, I'll tell my sweet, pretty mamma you did be good to her baby and took care of her all the time."

At that, Aunt Chloe strained the tiny form convulsively to her breast with a fresh burst of sobs, and looking up at Mildred with the great tears rolling down her cheeks, faltered out, "Oh, Miss

Milly, dey ain't gwine take my chile away and dis-separate ole Chloe from de las' ting she got lef' to lub in dis world?"

"Oh, mammy, no, no! Dey shan't; dey shan't!" cried the child, clinging about her neck in an almost wild fright. "Elsie won't go! Elsie will always stay wis her dear ole mammy!"

"No, no you are not to be parted," Mildred hastened to say. "Elsie, darling, your grandpa told me you were not. So don't cry, pet."

"Oh, Miss Milly, dat bressed news!" cried Aunt Chloe, smiling through her tears. "I's tank you berry much. Dere, dere, honey darlin', don' cry no mo'! I's an ole fool mammy to make you cry like dat."

The breakfast bell rang, and hastily removing the traces of the tears called forth by Aunt Chloe's narrative, Mildred obeyed the summons. Mr. Dinsmore seemed in excellent spirits, chatting in quite a lively strain all through the meal. He was enchanted with the place, he said, and intended, if agreeable to Mildred, to remain some weeks, believing that the change of scene and climate would prove beneficial to them both. Mildred assured him, her eyes sparkling with delight all the while, that she was perfectly willing to stay as long as it suited his convenience and pleasure.

"There are horses, carriages, and servants always at your command," he remarked. "A pleasure boat lies on the lakelet, too, so that you can go out on the water, ride, or drive whenever you wish."

"Oh, uncle, how nice!" she cried. "I shall enjoy it all greatly with little Elsie for a companion. And you will sometimes go with us when you have leisure, will you not?"

"I shall be most happy to," he said. "But I fear it will be but seldom that I can."

The family carriage was ordered at once, and the greater part of the morning was spent by Mildred, Elsie, and Aunt Chloe in driving from one lovely spot to another.

At little Elsie's request, they visited the family burial ground, and Mildred viewed with pensive interest the last resting place of her Cousin Horace's young wife, the "sweet, pretty mamma" of whom the baby girl so constantly prattled. The spot was beautiful with roses and many sweet-scented shrubs and flowers growing there, and Elsie and her mammy came daily there with love's offering in the shape of buds and blossoms gathered from the lawn and gardens, which they scattered with lavish hands over each lowly mound, always reserving the most and the loveliest for the grave of her whom they loved best.

There was seldom a day when the quarter was not visited also, Aunt Chloe taking her nursling from cabin to cabin to inquire concerning the welfare of the inhabitants and give to each the pleasure of the sight of the fair face that was so dear to them all.

Their devotion to her and the various ways in which they manifested it greatly pleased and interested Mildred. She was not long in discovering that they were exceedingly anxious in regard to the question whether both she—their idolized little mistress—and they were to be allowed to remain at Viamede.

Some of them even ventured in their great anxiety to inquire of the young lady visitor if she could tell them anything about these things.

She evaded the question so far as it referred to Elsie, feeling that she could not endure the sight of their grief when they should learn that they were to lose her. As to the other part, she said, truly, that she was ignorant, but she hoped there was no real danger.

She ventured at length to sound out her uncle on the subject, telling of the fears of the poor people. To her delight, she was given liberty to assure them that none would have to leave unless they became unruly or disobedient to orders.

She availed herself of this permission on her next visit to the quarter.

The communication was received with joy and gratitude, but there still remained the great fear that Mr. Dinsmore would carry away their darling. And this fear Mildred was powerless to remove.

She told Mrs. Murray about it, and the good woman confessed with tears, that she, too, was tortured with the fear of separation from "the sweet bairn she had learned to love as her very own," asking if Mildred knew whether that trial awaited her.

Mildred looked grieved and perplexed. "I only know," she said after a moment's hesitation, "that uncle intends taking his granddaughter home with him. Would you feel willing to leave Viamede, Mrs. Murray?"

"The bairn is far dearer to me than the place, though I hae spent mony o' the best years o' my life here," was the reply. "I wad gang onywhere sooner than part frae my bonnie bit lassie. I hae a mother's heart for her, Miss Keith, and hae often wanted to bid her call me by some dearer name than Mrs. Murray, but knowing the Dinsmores were a proud folk, I feared to offend. Now, I perceive it was well I refrained, since I learned frae Aunt Chloe that the grandfather was no a' all pleased that she spoke of Mr. Cameron as her uncle."

"No, he didn't seem to like it and told her not to do it again. But might that not be the jealousy of affection speaking?"

Mildred blushed as she spoke, almost ashamed — in view of Mr. Dinsmore's evident lack of love for the child — of making the suggestion.

"Affection!" repeated Mrs. Murray with a faint, incredulous smile. "I dinna see much in his manner toward the bairn that looks like it."

To this remark, Mildred had no answer save a deeper blush.

But at this moment, Mrs. Murray was summoned to a conference with Mr. Dinsmore in the library. She came back with a face full of great joy and thankfulness.

Mr. Dinsmore had received a letter that day from Mrs. Brown, the housekeeper at Roselands, saying that her health was failing. The physician recommended a change in climate, and she must resign her situation for a year or more.

Mr. Dinsmore now offered it to Mrs. Murray, and Aunt Phillis, an old servant in the family and very competent to the task, would be left in charge of the mansion here.

"I am very glad for both you and little Elsie," said Mildred. "Yet, I feel sorry for you, and for her, that you must leave this lovely spot. Is it not a trial?"

"I canna deny that it is, Miss," the housekeeper answered with a sigh, "for I hae lived at Viamede many years—years in which I hae seen much o' baith joy and sorrow. I had hoped to end my days here, but as the saintly Rutherford says, 'This is the Lord's lower house, and while we are lodged here we have no assurance to lie ever in one chamber but must be content to remove from one Lord's nether house to another, resting in hope that when we come up to the Lord's upper city, Jerusalem, that is above, we shall remove no more. Because then we shall be at home.'

"Ah, Miss Milly, what a joyous day it will be when we win there!"

CHAPTER
TWENTY-FOURTH

Must I leave thee, Paradise? Thus leave
Thee, native soul, these happy walks and shades,
Fit haunts of Gods?

—MILTON

MR. DINSMORE WAS, in the main, a kind-hearted man. Therefore, he felt a good deal uncomfortable in the prospect of the grief likely to be manifested by the five hundred servants working on the plantation, and particularly for the house servants, when called upon to part with little Elsie.

Both Mrs. Murray and Mildred had spoken to him of their strong attachment to the child, and his own observation had told him the same thing. He knew that they almost idolized her and would feel her removal as a heavy blow. Desirous to lighten the stroke, he determined to allow Elsie to make a farewell present to each and engaged Mildred and Mrs. Murray to assist her in preparing a list of suitable articles to be sent for. The child, knowing nothing of her grandfather's reasons for permitting this unusual outlay, was highly delighted.

It was Mr. Dinsmore's will that his plans regarding Elsie should be kept secret from her and the servants until near the end of his visit, still some weeks away.

Those weeks flew fast to Mildred, spent in a round of innocent, restful enjoyments, marred only by the knowledge that they must be so fleeting.

The day set for the departure from Viamede was drawing near when the sight of some of the needful preparations revealed the truth to the house servants. From them, the sad tidings spread to the field hands, causing great grief and consternation.

Elsie was perhaps the last to learn the truth. She was running through the lower hall one morning soon after breakfast, when Aunt Phillis suddenly caught her in her arms, and holding her tight, she covered the little fair face with kisses and tears.

"Why, Aunt Phillis, what's the matter?" asked the child, winding her small, plump arms about the woman's neck. "What makes you cry? Is you sick?"

"Oh, honey, darlin'," sobbed the almost disconsolate woman. "It's a heap wus dan dat! Dey's gwine to carry you 'way, bressed darlin' pet, 'way off Norf, where Aunt Phillis won't neber see yo' sweet face no mo'. Oh, dear! Oh, dear!"

"No, no!" cried the child, struggling to release herself. "Elsie's not goin' 'way, Aunt Phillis. Where's mammy? I want mammy!"

"Darlin', your ole mammy neber leave you!" Aunt Chloe said soothingly, evading the question she could not answer as she wished.

"Elsie doesn't want to go 'way!" sobbed the child. "Dis is Elsie's home; dis is Elsie's house. Elsie wants to stay here wis Aunt Phillis and all Elsie's people! Oh, mammy, mammy, does Elsie have to go?"

"Don't cry, honey; don't, darlin' pet. You won't have to go 'way from mammy. Mammy'll go 'long, too," was all Aunt Chloe could say.

The house servants were crowding around them, all weeping and wailing, and the little girl seemed quite inconsolable.

Mildred heard and came to the rescue.

"Darling child," she said, kneeling on the carpet by Elsie's side and softly stroking the beautiful hair. "You are going to your papa's home, and perhaps you will see him there before long. I think you will come back to Viamede someday."

At that, the little head was lifted, and a smile broke like a sunbeam through the rain of tears.

"Papa!" she exclaimed. "Will Elsie see her dear papa dere? Den I won't cry anymore!" And she wiped away her tears, saying, "Don't cry, Aunt Phillis and Aunt Sally, and de rest of you. My papa will bring me back again."

"Dat be a long time off!" muttered Aunt Phillis, shaking her head as she moved slowly away.

"Roselands, your grandpa's and papa's home, is a very pretty place," Mildred went on, still caressing the shining curls. "And there are little boys and girls there that Elsie can play with."

"Brothers and sisters for me?" asked the little one joyously.

"Your papa's brothers and sisters and nice, little playfellows for you," Mildred answered. "There is Enna, who is just a baby girl, only two years old."

"I's four. I's a big girl," put in the child.

"Yes, and Walter is past three, nearly as old as you. What nice playtimes you can have together."

"Yes, I want to take him a present, and one for the baby, and—what's dere names, de other children?"

Mildred went over the list, and the baby girl repeated her wish to take a gift to each.

"We will ask grandpa about it," Mildred said.

"Has dem children dot a mamma?" was the next query. That being answered in the affirmative, the wish was expressed that she, too, should be remembered with a very pretty present and that Cousin Milly would ask grandpa's permission for all these purchases.

Mildred took an early opportunity to do so.

"Who has put that nonsense into the child's head?" he asked in some vexation.

"No one, uncle. It was entirely her own idea, perhaps suggested by the thought of her proposed gifts to those she leaves behind."

"Very likely, but let her forget it. I do not want to encourage her to spend money upon my family."

"But her heart is very full of it, uncle, and I really think it would help to reconcile her to leaving Viamede. I'm afraid, uncle, that is going to be a hard trial for the little creature, for she dearly loves her home and her people, as she calls the servants."

"She will soon forget it all and perhaps like Roselands quite as well. Childish griefs are not lasting."

"But terribly hard while they do last, uncle. I am not so old yet as to have forgotten that."

"No?" he said with a smile followed by a sigh. "Ah, well, I'm sorry for the little thing, but I don't see how it can be helped."

"But you may lessen the trial by humoring her in this and everything else that is reasonable," persisted Mildred in her most persuasive tone.

"Well, well, if I must, I must, I suppose! What an excellent advocate you are. But really, I feel ashamed to allow it."

"Ah, uncle, it's your turn now," said Mildred, laughing. "I had mine in Philadelphia. But isn't Elsie rich enough to be allowed to spend such an amount on her own gratification?"

"Humph! What amount, pray? Ah, I have you there!" he added, laughing at her perplexed look.

"Not so fast, uncle!" she returned, brightening. "I can be definite. May she spend two hundred dollars for these gifts?"

"No."

"One hundred and fifty, then?"

"Hmm, I don't know. We'll see about it when we get to New Orleans."

"Then I may tell her that she is to be allowed to buy presents for them?"

"Yes. Now, please, don't make me commit myself any further."

After this, Mildred talked a great deal to the little girl about the children at Roselands, the games and romps she would have with them, what should be bought for them, and how pleased they would be with her gifts. She also told her all she was likely to see on her journey that would be new and interesting and how nice it was that Mrs. Murray and mammy were to go with her, grandpa, and Cousin Milly, and that the dear Savior and "her own sweet, pretty mamma" would be just as near her there in her new home as at Viamede.

It was thus she tried to tide the darling over the trial that awaited her in the sundering of the tender ties that bound her to the home of her early infancy.

Those were April days with the baby girl, from the time of Aunt Phillis's unfortunate revelation of what awaited her until the blow fell.

They were to leave in the morning, though not at a very early hour, and at Elsie's request, the field hands were excused from work for the half-day and directed to come up to the house soon after the family breakfast to say good-bye to their little mistress.

They gathered in a crowd in the rear of the mansion. The family party — Mr. Dinsmore, Mildred, Elsie, and Mrs. Murray — were assembled upon the back veranda, where stood a table piled with the goods to be distributed. The little girl sat beside it on her mammy's lap, Mildred and Mrs. Murray near at hand to give their assistance. The overseer, standing on the topmost step, called the roll, and each, coming forward in answer to his name, received a gift presented by the child herself and was allowed to kiss the small hand that bestowed it.

This was esteemed a great privilege, and many held the hand a moment, dropping tears as well as kisses upon it, heaping blessings on the head of the little fair one and pouring out their lamentations, also, over her approaching departure. At length, her tears fell so fast that her grandfather interfered, forbidding any further allusion to that subject on pain of having to receive their gifts from some other hand.

No one was neglected; no one had been forgotten. But each, from octogenarian no longer able or expected to work down to the babe of a few days, received a gift of substantial worth to him or her, after which came a liberal distribution of pies, cakes, candies, and fruits.

The baby girl dried her tears and even laughed right merrily more than once as she watched them at their feast. But her grief burst forth afresh and with redoubled violence when the time came for the final parting, and the house servants gathered, weeping, about her.

She embraced them in turn, again and again, clinging about their necks, crying. "Oh, Elsie can't go 'way and leave you! Elsie loves her own dear home and can't go 'way!" They strained the little form to their hearts with bitter wailing and lamentation.

To Mildred, the scene was heart-rending, and her tears fell fast. Mrs. Murray was scarcely less moved. Aunt Chloe was sobbing, and telltale moisture stood in Mr. Dinsmore's eyes.

"Come, come now," he said at length, speaking somewhat gruffly to hide his emotion. "We have had enough of this! There's no use in fretting over what cannot be helped. Elsie's father will be bringing her back one of these days, so dry your eyes, Aunt Phillis, and all of you. The boat is waiting, the captain wanting to be off. Are you quite ready, ladies?"

Receiving an answer in the affirmative, "Then let us go on board at once," he said, and he would have taken his little granddaughter in his arms, but Aunt Phillis begged the privilege of carrying her to the pier. Then with one last, long, clinging embrace, she resigned her to her nurse.

"Dere, honey darlin', dry yo' eyes and do'n cry no mo'. Wipe de tears away so you can see your home while we's goin' 'long past de orchard and fields," Aunt Chloe said, standing on the deck and lifting the child high in her arms. "An' look, pet, dere's all dem peeple, standing 'long de sho' to see de boat move off, and dat's de way dey'll stand and watch it when you and ole mammy comes back."

Yes, there they were, gathered in a crowd close to the water's edge, weeping and wailing, Aunt Phillis in the foreground wringing her hands, with big tears rolling fast down her cheeks.

The child saw and stretched out her arms to her with a cry of mingled love and distress. Then, as the boat swept onward, she turned and buried her face in her mammy's bosom.

Mildred saw it all through eyes dimmed with tears. "Don't cry, darling!" she whispered to Elsie. "Think about the time when your dear papa will bring you back. Now, lift up your head and look again at your beautiful home."

"Will my own papa bring Elsie back and live here wis me?" asked the little one, lifting her head as she was bidden and smiling through her tears as she gazed out over the lovely landscape.

"I hope so," Mildred said. "And you mustn't forget what a nice time we're going to have in New Orleans, buying the pretty things for the children at Roselands."

That was a wise suggestion and very helpful in cheering the sorrowful baby heart. In the discussion of the momentous and interesting questions of what those gifts should be and in what sort of places they would be found, she presently grew quite cheerful and animated.

A wonderful new world opened upon the baby eyes as they neared the city. She was filled with eager curiosity and delight, manifested in ways so entertaining and winsome, and by questions showing so much native wit, that her grandfather's heart warmed toward her. And, wherever they went, he found her attracting so much attention, by reason of her beauty, sweetness, and intelligence, that he grew proud of her in spite of himself.

Chapter Twenty-Fifth

Envy is but the smoke of low estate,
Ascending still against the fortunate.

—Lord Brooks

"Mama, what's the matter?" asked Adelaide Dinsmore as they sat at the breakfast table. Mrs. Dinsmore was reading a letter from her husband, and Adelaide had been studying her face all the while, noting the gathering frown upon the brow, the flushing cheek, and the compression of the lips that spoke of increasing anger.

"Matter? I was never so provoked in my entire life!" cried Mrs. Dinsmore, crushing the letter passionately in her hands, then tearing it into bits. "The idea of bringing that child here! And not merely for a visit, which would be bad enough, but to stay permanently. I don't know what your father can be thinking of! It seems it's not enough that I've been tormented with a stepson, but I must have a step—"

"Step what, mamma?" asked all three of the little girls present as she broke off abruptly, leaving her sentence unfinished.

"Nonsense! Be quiet, will you?" she answered angrily.

They waited a moment for her passion to cool, then Adelaide began again.

"What child, mamma? Is papa coming home and going to bring a child with him?"

"Yes, your brother Horace's child! You may as well know it first as last, I suppose."

Three pairs of eyes opened wide with amazement, three young voices crying out together, "Brother Horace's child! Why, mamma, what can you mean? We didn't know he had any. We never even heard that he was married!"

"Of course you didn't," said Mrs. Dinsmore, pushing away her plate. "And probably you never would if this child hadn't been stubbornly determined to live in spite of losing her mother before she was a week old.

"No, we were never proud of the match and had kept the thing quiet. But now it will be a nine days' wonder to the neighborhood, and the whole story will have to come out."

"Then you might as well tell it to us," was Adelaide's sage rejoinder. "Come, mamma, do, I'm dying of curiosity."

"It can be told in a few words," said Mrs. Dinsmore in a tone of wearied impatience. "Five years ago, Horace went on a visit to New Orleans, met an orphan girl of large fortune, fell in love with her, and persuaded her to marry him. The thing was clandestine, of course, for they were mere boy and girl. They lived together for two or three months, and her guardian, who had been away, came home, found it out, and was furious.

"He carried the girl off, nobody knew where. Your father sent Horace to college, and some months afterward we heard that the girl was dead and had left a baby. She's four years old now. The guardian is dead, and your father is bringing her home to live with us.

"There, I've given you the whole story, and I don't intend to be bothered with any more questions."

"But mamma," burst out the children, who had listened with breathless interest, "you haven't even told us her name or when they are coming!"

"Her name is Elsie, and they will be here in about a week. There now, not another question. I'm bored to death with the subject."

"Four years old. Why, she's just a baby," remarked Adelaide to her sisters. "Let's go tell mammy the news and that she's going to have another baby to take care of."

"No, she's not," said Mrs. Dinsmore sharply. "The child has a mammy of her own that's coming with her."

"What relation is she to us, Ade?" asked Lora.

"Who, the nurse? None to me, I'm sure," laughed Adelaide.

"You know I didn't mean that!" Lora retorted in a vexed tone.

"Why, we're aunts!" exclaimed Louise. "Now, isn't that funny? And mamma's already a grandmother! That's even funnier still!" she added with a burst of laughter.

Mrs. Dinsmore was in the act of leaving the room but turned back to say wrathfully, "No such thing!

The child is not related to me in the least. So, don't let me hear any more of that nonsense."

"Mamma's mad," laughed Louise, "mad enough to shake me, I do believe. She doesn't like to be thought old enough to be a grandmother."

"Maybe she isn't," said Lora. Horace was a pretty big boy when papa and mamma were married, wasn't he, Ade?"

"I can't remember before I was born," Adelaide answered teasingly.

"Well, if you don't know about anything but what has happened since you were born, you don't know much," Lora retorted with spirit. "But I'll go and ask mammy. She'll know, for she was here before he was born."

It was a lovely spring day, and from the windows of the breakfast room they could see Aunt Maria, the old woman who had been nurse in the family ever since the birth of Mr. Dinsmore's eldest child and whom they all called mammy, walking about under the trees in the garden with Baby Enna in her arms while Arthur and Walter gamboled together on the grass nearby.

"Ki, chillens! What's de mattah?" she exclaimed, pausing in her walk as the three little girls came bounding toward her in almost breathless excitement.

"Oh, mammy!" they cried as one. "Did you know that brother Horace was married and has a baby girl? And that papa's bringing her home to live?"

"Ki, chillens, what you talkin' 'bout?" returned the old woman incredulously. "You's tryin' to fool your ole mammy."

"No, no, mammy! It's all so. Mamma has just been telling us," and they went on to repeat substantially what they had just learned from their mother.

Aunt Maria was an intensely interested and astonished listener, and they had several others before their story was finished. Arthur and Walter came running up to ask what it was all about, and two or three servants also joined the little group.

"You looked pleased, mammy. Are you really?" asked Adelaide.

"To be sure I is, chile," returned the old nurse with a broad grin of satisfaction. "Marse Horace one ob my chillens, and I'll be mighty glad to see his little chile."

The news spread rapidly among the servants and formed their principal topic of conversation from that time till the arrival of their master and his charge.

On leaving the breakfast room, Mrs. Dinsmore bent her steps toward the nursery. She found it untenanted except for a housemaid who was engaged in putting it in order for the day.

"Go and tell Mrs. Brown that I wish to speak to her immediately," commanded the mistress, dropping into an easy chair.

"Yes, missus," said the girl, who disappeared to return shortly accompanied by the housekeeper.

"You have heard from Mr. Dinsmore?" remarked the lady inquiringly, addressing Mrs. Brown.

"Yes, ma'am. He writes that Mrs. Murray, the housekeeper at Viamede, has consented to take my place for the coming year."

"Yes, I'm afraid she won't suit me as well. It's a great pity you should have got such a notion in your head—I mean as to the necessity or desirability of going away. I don't think you'll find a healthier place anywhere else than Roselands."

"I've no fault to find with the place ma'am, but I need rest, the doctor says, from the care and—"

"Dr. Barton's full of notions!" interrupted Mrs. Dinsmore impatiently. "Well, you'll stay, I suppose, until Mrs. Murray learns from you about the ways of the house?"

"Yes, ma'am. Since you wish it."

Mrs. Dinsmore gave her orders for the day as usual, then said, "There's another thing, Mrs. Brown. You have probably heard that Mr. Dinsmore is bringing a child with him?"

"Yes, ma'am. He mentioned it in his letter to me, saying that a room must be got ready for her and her nurse."

"That is what I was coming to."

Mrs. Dinsmore arose and opened a door leading into an adjoining apartment.

"This room will serve very well. Have the trunks and boxes carried to the attic, the floor, paint, and windows washed, and a single bedstead, washstand, bureau, and two or three chairs brought in. Oh, and put up a white muslin curtain to the window."

"But, ma'am—Mrs. Dinsmore—" said Mrs. Brown, looking almost aghast at her employer.

"Well?" exclaimed the latter with sharpness.

"Excuse me, ma'am, but isn't—I understand that the little lady was Mr. Dinsmore's granddaughter and—and quite an heiress."

"Well, and supposing she is all that?"

"I beg pardon, Mrs. Dinsmore, but isn't the room rather small? Only one window, too, and I presume she's been used to—"

"It makes no difference what she's been used to, and you are presuming too far. You will be good enough to see that my orders are carried out at once," said Mrs. Dinsmore, sweeping from the room in her most dignified style. She turned at the door to add, "A cot bed can be put up here for the nurse and the door left open between at night," she said, then sailed majestically down the hall.

"Dear, dear, whatever will Mr. Dinsmore say to having his granddaughter put into such a hole as that!" exclaimed the housekeeper, half to herself and half to the housemaid. "Well, it can't be helped. I'll just have to do the best I can and tell him 'twasn't my fault. Sally, you go down and send up two of the boys to carry away these trunks, and tell Aunt Phoebe to heat a kettle of soft water for the scrubbing."

Mrs. Brown did her best. She had the room thoroughly cleaned, neatly papered and carpeted, had a set of pretty cottage furniture carried in, put a lace curtain to the window and looped it back with pink ribbon, made up the bed in the daintiest fashion, and on the day the travelers were expected to arrive, decorated the small apartment profusely with the loveliest and most fragrant flowers that could be found, transforming it into a bower of beauty.

Mrs. Dinsmore paid no attention at all to her proceedings, but the children watched them with interest, wondering the while that so mean a room had been selected for their little niece.

They were quite amused and gratified with the idea of being aunts and uncles, and if left to themselves, would have been disposed to welcome the little stranger warmly. But the slighting, sneering way in which their mother alluded to her and her mother's family presently impressed them with the idea that she was to be looked upon as an object of contempt, if not as a positive disgrace to the family.

They reasoned among themselves, the older ones at least, that probably Horace thought so, too, or he would have told them about her.

But when they saw the carriage bringing her, their father, and Mildred from the city rolling up the avenue, all this was forgotten, and they rushed to the door to meet them, filled with curiosity and delight.

There was a tumultuous embracing of their father and cousin, then they turned to look at the child.

What they saw was a small, fairy-like figure in the arms of her nurse, a delicate oval face tinted with the loveliest shades of pink and white and framed in by a mass of golden brown ringlets and lighted by a pair of eyes of the softest hazel, which were gazing half shyly, half eagerly at them.

"Oh, you darling, you pretty darling!" cried Adelaide, reaching her with a bound and giving her a vigorous hug and kiss. "Do you know that I'm your auntie? And don't you think it's funny?"

The embrace was instantly returned, a beautiful smile breaking over the sweet little face while the baby voice cooed, "Yes, Elsie loves you."

"Don't tease the child, Adelaide. Children, let her alone," said Mrs. Dinsmore, sharply.

But no one seemed to hear or heed. Children and servants had gathered round in quite a little crowd and were hugging and kissing and making much of her, examining her with as much curiosity as if she were a new specimen of humanity, calling her "Brother Horace's little girl" and "Massa Horace's baby" and remarking upon the beauty of her complexion, her eyes, her hair, and the tiny shapely hands and feet.

"They'll hae the bairn fairly puffed up wi' vanity, Miss Mildred!" exclaimed Mrs. Murray in a dismayed aside to our heroine.

"Never mind," whispered Mildred joyously. "I'm only too glad she should have such a welcome, the darling! And I don't believe it will hurt her in the least."

"There, children, and the rest of you, that will do," said Mr. Dinsmore with authority. "The child is tired from her long journey. Carry her to her room, Aunt Chloe, and let her have something to eat and a nap."

Aunt Chloe obeyed. Mildred hurried after to see the child comfortably established and then dress herself for dinner. Mrs. Brown invited Mrs. Murray to her new quarters, and Mr. Dinsmore, waiting only to give an order to his servant, hastened after the little girl and her attendant, following the sound of their voices, for the child was prattling to her mammy and Mildred, and they were answering her innocent questions and remarks.

"Dis my little missus's room?" Mr. Dinsmore heard Aunt Chloe exclaim in a tone of astonishment and contempt, as the little party guided by Sally, the housemaid, reached the door of the room selected by Mrs. Dinsmore.

He hurried forward. "What, this pigeonhole?" he exclaimed, turning wrathfully to the girl. "Who bade you bring the young lady, Mr. Horace's daughter, here to this room?"

"Missus tole de housekeeper fix dis room fo' de little lady, massa," replied the girl, trembling with great fright.

"You must have misunderstood her," he said. "This way, Aunt Chloe."

The room to which he conducted them adjoined that appropriated to Mildred and was equally large, airy, and cheerful, and equally well furnished.

Aunt Chloe surveyed it with a look of relief and satisfaction, and bidding her send Sally for whatever was wanted for the child, Mr. Dinsmore left them and went down to his wife.

She read displeasure in his countenance and drew out her handkerchief in preparation for her usual mode of defense.

"Pray, madam," he demanded in irate tone, "by whose orders was that cubbyhole prepared for the use of Horace's child?"

"That nice little room next to the nursery was the one selected by myself," she answered with dignity.

"Nice little room, indeed!" he returned with scorn. "Ten feet by twelve! That for one born in a palace and reared, thus far, in the lap of luxury!"

"Plenty good enough and big enough for old Grayson's grandchild!" observed his wife, turning up her aristocratic nose in supreme contempt.

"Madam, she is also my grandchild, and she is heiress in her own right to over a million."

Mrs. Dinsmore's look expressed at first great astonishment, then jealous rage and envy. "And the very incarnation of beauty!" she muttered between her clenched teeth. "What did you bring her here for—to cast our children into the shade? I hate her! What have you been doing? Where have you put her, then?

"In the blue room."

"The blue room! One of the very best in the house! The blue satin damask cushions of the chairs and sofas are so handsome and delicate! And to think of the sun being let in to fade them, a baby rubbing her shoes over them and scattering greasy crumbs on them. And that exquisite carpet! It's too trying for flesh and blood to stand!" and the handkerchief went up to her eyes.

"It's not worthwhile to distress yourself," he remarked coolly. "Her income is quite sufficient to allow it's being refurnished at double the cost every six months, if necessary."

"You ought to be ashamed of yourself, Mr. Dinsmore, throwing up her wealth to me in that style!" she sobbed.

Little Elsie was brought down to the drawing room after tea, Mildred leading her in while Chloe followed bearing a pasteboard box.

Fresh pangs of envy and jealousy assailed Mrs. Dinsmore at the sight of the little fair one, now rested and refreshed, beautifully and tastefully attired, and looking even more bewitchingly lovely than on her arrival.

Running to her grandfather, she asked coaxingly, "Please, drampa, may Elsie dive de fings now?"

"As well now as any time," he said not unkindly, and she ran back to Mildred, who had taken the box from Aunt Chloe and now opened and held it so that the child could handle the contents.

"This is the one for Enna's mamma," Mildred whispered, pointing to a jewel case. "I would give it first."

The small, white hands seized it, and the soft, hazel eyes glanced about the room till they rested upon the figure of a richly dressed lady in an easy chair. Then the little twinkling feet tripped across the room, and with a shy look up into the not too pleasant face, the case was laid in her lap, the baby voice lisping sweetly, "Please, Enna's mamma, Elsie wants to dive you dis."

Mrs. Dinsmore started with surprise, opened the case hastily, and seeing a very handsome gold bracelet lying there, condescended to smile and murmur a few words of thanks.

But the little one had not waited for them. Back to Mildred she ran in eager haste to finish the work of presenting her love tokens to these new-found relatives — a handsome gold ring to each of the three little girls, which were received with kisses, thanks, and exclamations of delight, and toys for the others, which seemed to give equal satisfaction.

CHAPTER TWENTY-SIXTH

Sweet beauty sleeps upon thy brow,
And floats before my eyes;
As meek and pure as doves art thou,
Or beings of the skies.

— ROBERT MORRIS

"DO YOU LIKE it, aunt?" asked Mildred, approaching Mrs. Dinsmore as she was in the act of clasping the bracelet on her arm.

"Yes, it's very handsome, but I think there might as well have been a pair of them."

"Ah!" returned Mildred with a smile directed toward Mr. Dinsmore. "Little Elsie would have been glad to make it so, but uncle held the purse strings and was inexorably determined that it should be but one."

"Just like him!" said the wife snappishly.

"My dear, I felt extremely mean in even allowing as much as I did to be spent upon my family," he said with a gravity that was almost stern.

"I don't see why you need feel so," she replied with irritation, "since you are sacrificing the comfort of your family, as you are, by taking her in."

"I must confess," he returned, "that I see no sacrifice about it. The child will not be the slightest

273

expense to us, but rather the reverse. Nor will her presence in the house add in the very least to your cares."

"The children seem well pleased with their gifts," Mildred remarked, giving him a cheery smile as she moved away toward them, gathering in a little throng about Elsie and amusing themselves by making her talk. They asked her questions, bidding her pronounce their names in turn with the prefix of aunt or uncle.

"You're the darlingest little thing that ever was!" Adelaide exclaimed, catching her in her arms and kissing her again and again.

"She's too pretty. Nobody will ever look at us when she's nearby. I heard mamma say so," muttered Louise discontentedly.

"Pooh! What's the use of talking in that way!" said Lora. "We can hide her upstairs when we want to be looked at."

"Of course," said Mildred, laughing, "and being such a mere baby, I don't think you need fear that she will prove a serious rival."

"I'm her uncle," remarked Arthur, drawing himself up with dignity. "Say Uncle Arthur again, baby girl."

"I isn't a baby," she said, smiling up into his face. "Elsie's a big girl now; Enna's de baby. Pretty baby! Elsie loves you!" she added, stroking Enna's hair.

"It's high time all of those children were in bed," said Mrs. Dinsmore from the other side of the room. "Aunt Marie, take Enna and the boys to the nursery."

Aunt Chloe, not slow to take a hint, picked up her nursling and followed the other woman, Elsie looking back and kissing her hand to her grandfather with a pleasant, "Goodnight, grandpa. Goodnight, Enna's mamma, and all de folks."

Mildred went with them to enjoy a little talk and play with the child, as had been her custom at Viamede, but she did not venture to stay long, lest Mrs. Dinsmore should be displeased about her absenting herself from the drawing room on the first evening after her return.

On going down again, she found Mr. Landreth there. He spent the evening and made himself very agreeable. Mildred was quite full of Viamede and its little heiress, and he seemed much interested in all she had to say about them.

Mr. Landreth was a favorite with Mrs. Dinsmore. She considered him an excellent match in point of wealth and family, possessed also of the added recommendations of a good education, polished address, and genial disposition.

He had been a frequent visitor to Roselands in the past months, and she had spared no pains to show off to him the attractions of her nieces and throw him as much as possible into their society, at the same time adroitly keeping Mildred in the background.

But the young man was sufficiently keen-sighted to see through her schemes, and while seemingly falling in with them, in reality reserved all his admiration for Mildred, who on her part was taken up with other interests and thought of him only as a pleasant acquaintance whose visits to the house meant nothing to her.

Mrs. Dinsmore had been disappointed by her

failure to secure him for one or the other of her nieces. But they were now both engaged, and having come to have as warm a liking for Mildred as it was in her selfish nature to entertain for anyone not connected with herself by ties of blood, she desired, as the next best thing, to bring about a match between her and Mr. Landreth.

But Mildred did not second her efforts, showing no particular preference for Mr. Landreth's society above that of any one of the half-dozen or more unmarried gentlemen who frequented the house.

She treated them all courteously but gave encouragement to none, seeming far more interested in little Elsie and in her studies, which had been almost discontinued during her stay at Viamede but had been taken up again with renewed zeal directly upon her return to Roselands.

But Mr. Landreth was not to be discouraged. He paid court to Elsie, learning soon to love the little creature for her own sweet sake and managed, after a time, to associate himself with several of Mildred's pursuits.

The time had now arrived when, according to the original plan, Mildred was to return home, and those who loved her there were looking forward with eager impatience for her coming.

But Mr. Dinsmore wrote to her parents, entreating that he might be allowed to keep her some months longer and bringing forward several cogent reasons why his request should be granted. Mildred was improving in health, making the best use of every opportunity to perfect herself in her accomplishments, was a most pleasant companion to himself and wife, and ought not to be permitted to undertake the long journey alone, while at present no suitable escort could be found.

The parents carefully weighed his arguments, and for their child's sake, finally gave consent, albeit somewhat reluctantly.

Mildred was both glad and sorry, having a yearning desire for home and its dear occupants but at the same time feeling that the parting from wee Elsie would be very sad, so tender was the attachment that had sprung up between herself and the motherless babe.

Pity was a large element in Mildred's love for the child and that increased as the weeks and months rolled on. Both the grandfather and the young uncles and aunts, yielding gradually to Mrs. Dinsmore's baleful influence, treated her with less kindness and consideration, while Mrs. Dinsmore's tyranny was such that not unfrequently Mildred could scarcely refrain from expressing violent indignation.

The child was not subjected to blows, but angry looks and harsh words and tones that to her sensitive spirit were worse than blows would have been to a more obtuse nature were plentifully dealt out to her. Ridicule, sneers, and snubs were also the norm.

And there was no respect shown to her rights of property. The other children might rob her of her toys, books, and pictures with entire impunity if she ventured to carry them outside her own room, Mrs. Dinsmore averring that if she showed them, and so excited a desire for them in the hearts of her children, she deserved to lose them.

"She is quite able to afford to present them with anything they want," she would add, "and I am not going to have them tormented with the sight of pretty things that are to be refused them."

Elsie was so unselfish and generous that, as a usual thing, she could be easily induced to give even what she highly valued. But to have violent hands laid upon her possessions and forced from her outraged her sense of justice, and though she seldom offered much resistance, it often cost her many bitter tears.

She was a careful little body who never destroyed anything, and her loving nature made her cling even to material things, in some instances, which she had owned and amused herself with for years. An old dolly that she had loved and nursed from what was to her time immemorial was so dear and precious that no new one, however beautiful and fine, could possibly replace it. And a living pet took such a place in her heart from the first—a tame squirrel that she had brought with her and a white dove given her by Mr. Landreth soon after her arrival.

But all these were taken from her. The doll had to be resigned to Enna, the dove to Walter, and the squirrel to Arthur.

There was a short struggle each time, then she gave it up and sobbed out her sorrow in her mammy's arms or on Mildred's sympathizing bosom.

"Oh, Elsie wants to go back to her own dear home!" she would cry. "Can't Elsie go back? Must Elsie stay here, where dey take her fings all away?"

Mildred, at first, hoped her uncle would interfere, but no, he did not enjoy contention with his wife, and, like many another man, could not understand how things of value so trifling in his sight could be worth so much to the child.

He was willing to replace them and thought it only ill temper and stubbornness when she refused to be comforted in that manner.

It was a sore trial to the three hearts in the house that loved her so dearly, but all they could do was to soothe her with caresses and assurances of their love and of the love of Jesus. They told her that if she bore her trials with meekness and patience, returning good for evil to those who used her so ill, it would be pleasing to Him.

Mildred would talk to her of her papa, too, and the happy times she would have when he came home — and how he would pet and love her.

"For surely" she reasoned with herself, "he cannot possibly do otherwise when he sees how sweet and lovely she is."

The prospect seemed to give the little one intense pleasure, and she would often ask to be told "'bout de time when Elsie's dear papa will come."

She would watch her grandfather, too, as he cradled his little ones, with a wistful longing in her sweet hazel eyes that brought sad tears to Mildred's eyes and made her heart ache.

CHAPTER TWENTY-SEVENTH

Wooing thee, I found thee of more value
Than stamps in gold, or sums in sealed bags.
And 'tis the very riches of thyself
That now I aim at.

— SHAKESPEARE

EARLY IN JUNE, the Dinsmore family repaired to the seashore, taking Mildred with them and also little Elsie and her mammy.

The whole summer was spent at watering-places, and Mr. Landreth was generally one of their party.

Mildred enjoyed it—the time spent at the seashore, especially, very much in a quiet way, taking no part in the gaieties of the fashionable set but delighting in walks and drives along the beach and in boating and bathing.

Elsie was fond of a morning stroll on the beach with "Cousin Milly," Aunt Chloe being always at hand to carry her pet when the little feet grew tired. Mildred was never averse to the companionship of the sweet child and never in too great a haste to accommodate her pace to that of the little one, or to stop to examine and explain whatever excited her curiosity, or let her pick up seaweed, shells, and pebbles.

Sometimes the older children joined them, and occasionally Mr. Landreth also. Later in the day, he was almost sure to be Mildred's companion, unless she contrived to elude him.

This she attempted quite frequently toward the latter part of the summer, declining his attentions whenever she could without positive rudeness.

At first, he would not believe it was by design, but at length he could no longer shut his eyes to the fact, and much disturbed and mortified, he determined to seek an explanation. He must know what was her motive — whether aversion to his society or fear that he was trifling with her. If it were the latter, that fear should speedily be removed, and he would tell her what was the sober truth—that he esteemed and admired her above all the rest of her sex and that he would be supremely happy if she would consent to be his wife.

They and their party had left the seashore for a fashionable resort among the mountains, where they had now been for a fortnight or more and where they had found the elder Mr. Landreth and his wife established for the season.

Mildred set out for a walk one morning directly after breakfast, taking Elsie and her nurse with her.

They found a cool, shady spot beside a little brook at the foot of a hill where the grass was green, and a rustic seat under a spreading tree invited rest.

They sat down, and Elsie amused herself with throwing pebbles and bits of bark into the water.

"Aunt Chloe," Mildred said presently, "I want to

climb this hill, for the sake of the view. So I will leave you and Elsie here. I don't intend to be gone long, but if she gets tired of waiting, you can take her back to the house, and I will follow later."

So saying, she tripped away back to the road, made her ascent, and seated herself upon a log at a spot which commanded a fine view of the mountain, hill, and vale. Taking out her drawing materials, she was about to sketch the scene, when a voice addressed her.

"Good morning, Miss Keith. I am happy to have come upon you just now, and alone.

"I'm quite out of breath with climbing the hill," the voice went on, as Mildred, turning her head, recognized Mrs. Landreth, responded to her greeting, and made room for her on the log. "Thank you. Yes, I will sit down here beside you, for I want to rest and to have a little talk with you."

"I am at your service, Mrs. Landreth," Mildred said, closing her sketchbook and recalling as she did so her companion's formerly expressed opinion that such employment was a sinful waste of time. She fully anticipated a lecture on the subject.

However, the good woman's thoughts were, at the moment, too full of a more important theme to allow her to so much as notice with what the girl had busied herself.

"My dear," she began, "I have a strong liking and high respect for you, because you seem to me sincerely desirous to do right and live in a Christian way, according to your light. You are merrier, of course, in your dress than I can think consistent, but we don't all see alike. I should be rejoiced to receive you into the family if that might be without the danger to you—spiritually—which it involves."

Mildred rose, her cheeks burning and her eyes flashing wildly.

"When I have shown my desire to enter your family, Mrs. Landreth, it will be time enough to—"

"Ah, my dear, my dear, you quite misunderstand me," interrupted the older lady. "Except for your own sake and your duty as a Christian to marry only in the Lord, I should be delighted. And I've never felt at all sure that Charlie could get you, but I see plainly that he wants you, so it seemed my duty to warn you not to take him."

Mildred was very angry. Drawing herself up to her full height and speaking with hauteur, "Excuse me, madam," she said, "I will venture to remind you that unasked advice is seldom acceptable, and I will add that it is especially unpalatable when it involves the meddling with matters too delicate for even the most intimate friends to allude to uninvited."

"What a temper! I begin to think you are none too good for him after all," grimly commented Mrs. Landreth, rising in her turn. "Good morning, miss," she said, stalking away down the hill while Mildred dropped upon the grass, hiding her face in her hands, and indulged in a hearty cry.

It was a mixture of emotions that brought the tears in those plentiful showers. Anger burned still in her breast, yet at the same time she was bitterly remorseful on account of it, sorry and ashamed that she had so disgraced her Christian profession, bringing reproach upon the Master's cause. Ah, what meant the pang that meddling woman's words had caused? Could it be fear that duty called her to resign that which had become very dear to her heart? Alas, yes! It cried out with a yearning, passionate cry for this love that she must reject, if indeed it was offered her.

Did he indeed love her? Oh, what joy! What bliss! But, oh, the bitter anguish if she must put that cup of joy aside untasted! How could she? Yet how dare she do otherwise? The Bible did speak of marrying only in the Lord. It did say, "Be ye not unequally yoked together with unbelievers."

Someone knelt on the grass at her side, gently lifted up her head and took her hands in his.

"Don't, darling. I cannot bear to see tears in those dear eyes. I know all—I met her, and she told me. How dare she so wound your delicacy! But it is true that I love you; yes, a thousand times better than she can even imagine! And it is also true that I am utterly unworthy of you. But, Mildred, dearest, sweetest, best of women, give me a little hope, and I will try to become all you can ask."

She could not speak. She tried to hide her blushing face and to withdraw her hands, but he held them fast and continued to pour out earnest pleadings and passionate expressions of love and devotion.

"Oh, I cannot!" she stammered at last. "I'm afraid she is right. Not, oh, not that I am any better than you! But—but we are traveling different roads, and 'how can two walk together except they be agreed?'"

"I would never interfere with your religion," he said. "I know it is different from that which makes my poor uncle's home the most desolate place on earth. Oh, Mildred, think that you may be the saving of me! I am willing to walk in your road if you will show me the way. I will even join the church at once if that will satisfy you."

She looked up wistfully into his face. "Ah, Charlie—Mr. Landreth—is that your idea of what it is to be a Christian? Ah, it is more, much more.

"'With the heart man believeth unto righteousness'—meaning he gets the righteousness of Christ put upon him, imputed to him, while holy living proves the reality of the change, the saving nature of faith—'and with the mouth confession is made unto salvation.'

"Do you not see that conversion must come before joining the church?"

"I don't understand these things," he said, "but I am willing to learn. Oh, Mildred, be my wife, and you may lead me whither you will!"

She shook her head sorrowfully, tears stealing down her cheeks.

"I am too weak and too ready to stray from the path myself. I am too easily led by those I—"

"Love?" he whispered eagerly, bending over her, as she paused in confusion. "Oh, Mildred, darling, say the sweet word! You do love me! You do! I see it in your dear eyes, and I will never despair. But speak the word, dearest. Once, just once!"

"Oh, Charlie!" she groaned, covering her face. "I should learn to love you too well to bear the thought that we were not to spend eternity together."

THE END

The Original Elsie Classics

Elsie Dinsmore

Elsie's Holidays at Roselands

Elsie's Girlhood

Elsie's Womanhood

Elsie's Motherhood

Elsie's Children

Elsie's Widowhood

Grandmother Elsie

Elsie's New Relations

Elsie at Nantucket

The Two Elsies

Elsie's Kith and Kin

Elsie's Friends at Woodburn

Christmas with Grandma Elsie

Elsie and the Raymonds

Elsie Yachting with the Raymonds

Elsie's Vacation

Elsie at Viamede

Elsie at Ion

Elsie at the World's Fair

Elsie's Journey on Inland Waters

Elsie at Home

Elsie on the Hudson

Elsie in the South

Elsie's Young Folks

Elsie's Winter Trip

Elsie and Her Loved Ones

Elsie and Her Namesakes